CONQUERED

A Paranormal Romance Novel

By
Sandy L. Rowland

PUBLISHED BY
Sandy L. Rowland

Conquered © 2012 Sandy L. Rowland

Editing by Kelli Ann Morgan

Cover Design © Kelli Ann Morgan
Inspire Creative Services
www.inspirecreativeservices.com

Interior book design by
Bob Houston eBook Formatting
http://about.me/BobHouston

ABOUT CONQUERED

Claiming a mate on conquered Earth is driving alien vampire, Rafe, insane… literally.

He's lost his comrade to madness and has sworn against suffering the same fate. Time is out for the ruler of the western quadrant and any female will do.

Spunky reporter, Pepper Morgan, has lost friends, her mother, and a fiancé to the devastating plague that ravished Earth before the vampire's subjugated them. Desperate to reunite with her captured father, she throws herself on Rafe's mercy.

Now Rafe and Pepper find themselves bound by more than desperation and blood, but also secrets that have the power to enslave humanity and threaten vampire survival. Can they overcome their inner demons and learn to trust each other, before it's too late?

DEDICATION

It's been a long, hard road getting here, but worth the effort. I'm better for it. My family says that I'm happier since I began the process of writing a novel. It's true. I'm more content, but it's not just the writing, it's the support of my loving husband, Rob, who put up with the dining room table cluttered with pages, and my nose stuck in a book or at the computer until late at night. And to my children for loving me through my frustrations, you helped me focus. To my daughter, Tiffany, for doing great content editing, thank you for making me slow down. To my original critique buddy, Clancy, who bravely waded through the early drafts that made her pen run dry of red ink. Thank you. And to Ralph Morris, for his superior critique services.

To the Utah chapter of Romance Writers of America for making the dream of publication real and attainable, you are my heroes. And to all those readers who believe they can overcome their struggles and gain love, this is for you.

CONQUERED

By
Sandy L. Rowland

CHAPTER ONE

Earth

Twenty-years in the future.

It shouldn't happen like this. A man has a right to his dignity. Rafe Nucretah narrowed his sharp eyes in the moonless autumn night and surveyed the damage. Utah's southern desert stretched before him, parched red dirt and wild sage littered with massacred flesh. He strode toward a rumpled mass on the sandy ground. His jaw clenched as he stared into the tender face of a murdered child, five years old maybe, round cheeked with golden curls. Human. Her sweet visage reminded him of his sister. He swallowed and turned away.

"Dante," Rafe croaked, then coughed to clear what lodged in his throat. "How many?"

His younger brother stood tall and slender, dressed in the jet-black uniform of an Enforcer. Dante's dark eyes flashed with rage "Eighteen. Three are my men, the rest human."

Rafe shook his head against the loss. *How could this happen?*

"Were there signs of the madness?" Dante's dark gaze narrowed hard as obsidian.

"None that I detected last week." Rafe's stomach knotted. Surely some nervous laughter and rambling didn't mean anything. *My recent fatigue is nothing. I'm not at risk. Not yet.* "Where is Hebric?"

Dante moved closer, silent. "Skulking around The Devil's Garden. Follow the trail of blood with caution. I know he's your friend, but I doubt he'll recall that fact before he tries to fry you with his Nova sword."

Friend. When the *Rosh* madness hit, there were no friends, but Rafe owed Hebric his life. Frustration grew in him, rising like a demon. Too late to save his childhood friend, the best he could manage was a dignified end, a warrior's death in battle.

Rafe swore to himself in the ancient language. This shouldn't happen. Hebric was close to a thousand-years-old, but he should've had fifty years before the madness hit. *I should have that much.*

Pressure crushed Rafe's chest. The thought of killing the man he loved as a brother brought the bitter taste of bile into his mouth, combining with the reality before him. If Rafe failed, Hebric would have his name and deeds expunged from the annals, as if he'd never existed: the worst fate possible.

Rafe clenched his fists. *I will not fail.* Hebric must die with his weapon in hand to maintain his place of honor and continue in the other realms. Rafe determined he'd give him that chance.

Rafe lifted his nose to the air. The coppery smell of blood mingled with death to fill his senses, familiar and unwelcome. For a moment, Rafe's thoughts lay chained on another world. His heart pounded and he shook himself violently back to Earth. He breathed through the wrenching memory.

"I have the Enforcers cleaning up this mess. Bram won't arrive for another week," said Dante. "If the media gets a hold of it this time, there will be real trouble."

"Trouble? A tame word for insurrection. If the rebels hear of it, I doubt if even Talon can dissuade revolt. Our existence depends on maintaining control." Rafe felt the weight of decision and rolled his shoulders. If humans learned the truth, they'd fight, and every drop of their blood was precious. "Don't worry. I'll post the dead as having transferred to Kivron, as usual. I can handle the heat from the High Council." Rafe clenched his teeth. He hated the politics, the lies, and the senseless end of life.

Rafe pulled his Neutron Eliminator from the loop on his belt and followed the carnage across the sun-baked ground. His black leather boots crunched against sand over stone until he stopped at the next rise, grateful his battle suit hid him in the darkness. Even crazed, Hebric would be difficult to overcome. "This way." He beckoned Dante and the Enforcers to back him up, and pushed down the despair threatening his focus.

The trail loomed ahead, towering rock walls with scrub oak eerily gray in the night. The cool desert wind rustled his hair and Rafe brushed it back from his wary eyes. His claws lengthened in preparation. Rafe knew the vampire's talents and steeled himself against what might lie ahead, waiting for him in the shadows.

The Enforcers positioned themselves around the sandstone pillars with their jagged outcroppings. Rafe took a few steps in the direction of the sizzle from a Nova sword and the stink of burning flesh. "Hebric, come out and let's talk." Concern thickened Rafe's tone as he stalked nearer.

"No. I'm busy," rasped a voice ahead and to Rafe's right.

Rafe's fangs lengthened. "Too busy for an old friend? It's Rafe Nucretah. We were in school together and fought side by side in the war on Kivron. You remember?" He crept forward.

"Rafe?"

"Yes." He skulked around a twisted cedar, the woodsy scent masking his own. "I've come to visit." Feelings of sorrow, love, and pity warred within him. He had to remain sharp and tamp down the uncomfortable emotions.

Another sizzle from the Nova sword. "Are you hungry? Join me for a meal." Hebric's voice thinned on the breeze.

The stench of charred flesh wafted toward Rafe. He cringed, fearing what he'd find. "Don't go to any trouble on my behalf. We can talk about the time you saved my life. You were the bravest of all." Rafe slipped through the rock passage.

"I remember. It's no trouble. I just sliced off a juicy limb. Join me."

"*Silch.*" Rafe sprinted past a boulder, tore through the passage, and halted before a cleft in the rock. He peered in.

There, with his back against the rough sandstone sat Hebric, his large powerful build wearing his charcoal dress uniform. His fangs dripped red as he held up his own severed leg. "It's fresh," he wheezed.

Rafe wanted to turn away from the morbid sight, but couldn't. How could he bring his friend to a respectful end if he couldn't fight? The madness had brought a valiant warrior to this, and it tore at Rafe's heart. His comrade and trusted friend, lost to him. He fought back the tears stinging behind his eyes as he cautiously stepped closer. Bile rose and Rafe swallowed it, willing his mouth to smile. "I see that."

He moved beside his friend, picked up the sword lying in the dirt, and held it out to Hebric. He ignored it and continued to stare at the flesh in his hands. Rafe swallowed hard, accepted the juicy limb from his friend, and then pressed the weapon into Hebric's palm.

"Fight me." Rafe waved his own weapon above Hebric's head.

"You want games? I'm tired, Rafe. Perhaps I've eaten too much. After a nap." Hebric's head bobbed and his eyelids lowered to slits.

"No! Take a swipe at me." Rafe taunted him, desperate to get him to act.

"Later. Aren't you hungry?" Hebric's gray eyes opened briefly.

Dante and the rest circled around Rafe, disgust and grim acceptance stamped on their faces. Hebric grimaced, and his pale brows furrowed. "You brought company. I don't believe one leg will be enough." He dropped the Nova sword and his arm fell at his side.

Rafe's throat closed as he hunkered down beside his friend. Hebric was dead. Grief twisted his gut. "I'm sorry, old friend. I've failed you," he murmured. "I've eternally failed you."

The crimson flood coated the dirt and soles of Rafe's black boots, making them slide against the rock as he turned toward Dante.

"He wasn't yet one thousand," said Dante, his skin paler than usual.

"No."

Dante set his shadowed gaze on Rafe. "He waited too long."

"We all know the risk of nearing a thousand years. Hebric thought he had time." Rafe schooled his emotions and watched understanding burden his brother's face.

"He was two years younger than you," whispered Dante.

"Are you worried for my sanity? Don't be. I'm not Hebric. I'll be safe after I claim a mate." Rafe rubbed the back of his neck. "Hebric admitted to being too choosy."

"But no unattached male is safe from the madness once he reaches one thousand, not even you."

Rafe winced inwardly. "I'm well aware of my situation." He looked on Hebric's mangled body. "I'll take care of it."

# # #

Three nights since the carnage in the desert and Rafe still couldn't shake the vile images from his mind. He'd done all in his power to save Hebric's honor and had failed. The memory of Kivronian blood still lay heavy in his nose. When he'd returned home that night, he'd had his battle suit and blood stained boots destroyed. He couldn't look on them without seeing his own destruction.

The signs of madness were becoming impossible to ignore, clouded thinking, occasional confusion, and the slight impairment of his natural abilities were only the beginning. So far, he'd kept his illness hidden. But how long could his gift for logic withstand the insanity that had shredded Hebric's mind? *I must act tonight.*

He dressed in a charcoal suit, shirt, and crimson tie. Red was the sacred color for loss. Now, his tie was the only respect he could allow without drawing attention. Through three nights of mourning in secret, Rafe had worn the red robe in his rooms as he burned all correspondence and memorabilia from his friend. Hebric's multiple offences, succumbing to madness, slaughtering humans, the source of Kivronian life, and then to die as he did—disgraced without redemption, made it an offense to whisper his name. As of dawn today, Hebric never existed. Tears welled up, but Rafe fought the display. *Enough.* Silent memories were all he had left of the man he'd loved as a brother.

Tonight, he'd act before he fell to the same fate. Rafe's heart wasn't in the search for a mate, but he refused to let Hebric's death count for nothing. *I'll do my duty in your honor—and live.*

Rafe found Dante in the dining room, sipping a glass of blood from a crystal goblet. Normally, Rafe enjoyed the conversations shared in this room of dark wood and yellow walls, but not on this night. Taking a deep breath, Rafe broached the uncomfortable subject. "It's been scheduled. I'll secure a mate tonight."

Dante sat back in the heavy oak chair and studied his brother. "You've decided on a human female, then. Who is she? The South American Ambassador's daughter or the attaché from China?"

After the ache of Hebric's loss, Rafe understood his brother's concern for him, but it didn't ease his task. "There are plenty of attractive females on Earth. For once, my position as

Governor isn't important, survival is. I won't take months to woo an appropriate prize. I should've taken care of this before now. I knew my time was drawing short. I just...."

Hebric's blood, darkening the sand invaded Rafe's mind and he shook his head against it. "I'll make a claim."

"Do you have one in mind?"

"No, but since waiting to win one of our own females in the lottery isn't an option I can afford, I'll make due with a human." Rafe felt desperation churning his insides. He couldn't chance putting it off, couldn't meet the same end as his comrade. Another violent twist of his heart made Rafe rub his stinging eyes with his fingers. "I'll have a bride."

Dante's jet-black brows traveled up. "You can't mean to bind yourself to a female you barely know. I realize the situation has been difficult and the loss, great, but this is for eternity. Couldn't you wait until our brother and sire return?"

"Don't worry, Bram will understand and our sire will be relieved it's done. I'm taking precautions. The women will be fully vetted by Match Maker Registry. Many females seek Kivronian husbands and will accept if I offer. It's been done by others." Rafe leaned forward and locked eyes with Dante. "Better to be bound to a stranger and live, than face insanity and be expunged from the annals. I mean to survive."

Within the hour, Rafe sped down the darkened highway through the desert, lit only by the stars, and the headlights of his black Bentley. The Kivronian vehicles he owned were faster, but he enjoyed the vintage car. Control rested solely in his hands, rather than the voice-activated computer. *Hebric hates this car. Hated.*

His friend's death sliced through him like a Nova sword. Rafe grimaced, pressed harder on the accelerator and flew past the cremation facility. His comrade's torso had turned to ash within hours. The remnants scattered to the winds while his head had sat prominently displayed to ridicule for three nights. Even his skull had been ground to dust by now. Hebric had been valiant, a warrior of the first order. He deserved better.

Rafe pulled himself from the painful thoughts and focused on the task at hand. Claiming a mate should be a joyful undertaking, but not under the present circumstances. The binding would stunt madness, but not cure it. Only his mate's love would hold such power. Even if she did grow to love him enough, the binding would end his chance of having children. Humans couldn't bear their young. It's the reason Hebric had put off taking a mate, hoping to win a Kivronian female in the lottery. They'd spoken of it often since invading Earth. The joy of little ones, teaching them to fight, making sure they grew into valiant warriors, true, brave, and strong. It's also the reason Rafe had procrastinated. *That future is gone.* His fingers tightened on the wheel.

The goal of claiming a female would have to coincide with business. He had a sector to run, and the nasty business of covering up the massacre of eighteen people. A statement had been sent to the media the next day. The immediate transfer of humans to his home planet rarely occurred, most often when an accidental loss of life made it a necessary ploy. He hoped the rebels believed it. His jaw tightened. Only a direct order from the High Council could make him engage in such deceit. Duty and survival of his people made his compliance imperative. But he didn't like it.

At least, the issue of claiming a mate would be done by evening's end. His assistant had scheduled a parade of eligible young women for Rafe to peruse between meetings. *Ridiculous. What kind of person would degrade herself in that way?* He couldn't imagine, and didn't relish finding out. "Some social climber or a girl desperate to further her career," he grumbled.

Rafe scowled. The tires screeched and threw red sand as he

took the turn into town. He'd known one day he'd likely have to claim a human. There were few Kivronian females left after the civil war, but the High Council claimed most and dangled the rest before their males in the Lottery. Chances of winning against such odds were miniscule.

Humans were illogical, fragile, and their culture confusing. And now he must bind himself to such a creature? Rafe chafed at the idea. He demanded order. Lived and breathed the neat, controlled existence of the military. No matter the difficulties, he'd make it work. *I'm in control of the situation.*

Rafe halted before the government complex and killed the engine. He would accomplish his objective, find a female who wasn't overly annoying, claim and bind her. With his superior senses and intellect, he should be able to pick a suitable mate, even in Red Rock, Utah.

# # #

Pepper sat poised in Governor Nucretah's waiting area, her laptop computer balanced on her skirt-clad thighs as she typed notes for her latest assignment. Landing an interview with Governor Rafe Nucretah was a coup. She'd been trying for months. Though he'd agreed, she'd shown up every night for the last three, sitting in the hall, trying to get in to see the most powerful, and reportedly, devastatingly handsome, alien vampire in the Western Quadrant. Tonight he was available, and Pepper had finally been allowed past the front desk. She refused to leave without seeing him.

Months ago, Pepper had graduated from writing the food section of the *Red Rock Times* to fulfill her dream job: investigative reporter. She'd longed to sink her teeth into reporting on political corruption and to tear it wide open. The public had a right to know. Even though, after the alien take-over there wasn't much a human could do to change things. Still, knowledge was power. Humanity needed information, and Pepper Morgan was just the girl to give it to them.

This assignment was nothing special. Yet another group of humans had been transferred to the planet, Kivron. The real story was the man who authorized the transfers. That's what she'd told her editor, but Pepper had begged for the assignment for other reasons than a story.

Worry over her father kept her up at night. Her concern had grown until it had possessed her thoughts and had railed at her every waking moment. Information didn't cause her anxiety, but the lack of it. Pepper trusted her gut. She hadn't heard from her father, except for the few letters that came by way of the inter-galactic transporter, and they were infrequent. *So unlike him. Something is very wrong.*

Six months ago, he'd been transferred. "Shanghaied, was more like it," she muttered to herself. She'd returned home from work to find an official letter on the kitchen table next to her father's blue coffee cup. *The services of Dr. Ben Morgan were required for an indefinite interval.* His clothes and essentials were gone, but he'd left the sweater she'd made him last Christmas. Little things like that gnawed at her. His favorite ratty sneakers cluttered the floor of his closet. Those things she could attribute to the speed of his leaving, but not the photo of her mom. He always kept it next to his bed. He'd have taken that—if he could have.

Her father was a renowned biologist and useful to the aliens. She was proud of him. His search for a cure for the ruthless plague that had devastated Earth's population had taken most of his time. He would have forgotten to eat, if she hadn't shoved a plate of food under his nose. He would tease her about her cooking. The toast was too brown and the eggs were too wet. She blinked back moisture and wiped her cheek. He'd eat every crumb.

Her mother had succumbed to the disease at its height, ten

years ago. Civilization had dissolved into chaos as the body count had mounted. Pepper shuddered. Fearful thoughts of those days haunted her. Earth had become a war zone. Her stomach knotted. She'd been fifteen. There were no words dark enough to capture those months of loss and devastation.

And then the aliens came.

Kivronian medicine had proved their salvation. Working with her father, the deaths ended and society reordered. Humanity owed its life to the vampires—and the invaders meant to collect. She closed her laptop and fisted her hands in her lap. *At least when Mom died, I had the chance to say, "Goodbye".*

A gaggle of young women fluttered into the waiting area, all well dressed and dripping sophistication.

"Ladies, I'm Celeste, Mr. Nucretah's assistant. Make sure we have your current information so we can contact you."

Pepper studied the slight, coal haired vampire. She had the most unusual silver eyes. Her blood red lips, set against bone white flesh, might have been appealing, if she didn't make Pepper's skin crawl. *Call it intuition or a hunch, but there's something creepy about that woman.* After three nights, Pepper thought she'd seen everyone, but not Celeste. Apparently, if

Nucretah didn't show up, neither did his assistant. *Rough life.*

Turning her focus to the women, Pepper could see that any one of them could have been a model or a beauty queen, if those industries had still existed. Who were they? Too refined for hookers, and too well dressed to need a job, these women looked like exotic jewels, born to adorn a powerful man's arm.

Pepper ran her hand over her navy wool skirt. The suit was well made, and still in decent shape for being second hand, but her white blouse was almost new. She pulled a loose thread from her jacket and sat up a little straighter.

Watching the group with rapt attention, Pepper continued her speculation. They wore make-up and jewelry. A few bothered to style their hair in a sleek Kivronian knot, a sort of French twist that bared their necks. Alluring to vampires.

Most humans couldn't afford cosmetics and Pepper went about fresh-faced. Her dad used to say her skin didn't need help and her cheeks were blessed with a natural rosy glow. *Oh Dad, how I miss you.* One of the beauties wore false lashes. Bambi would kill to have eyes like those. Pepper sighed. *Who am I kidding*? Her clump of auburn hair was too thick and hung to her waist. Her eyes weren't anything spectacular. She should be grateful she wasn't competing with those goddesses. What were they doing here?

Being the investigative reporter she was, Pepper marched up to the girl with the lashes, who wore a cream silk dress, and began interrogating. "Lovely dress. Is this for a photo shoot?" Pepper waved her arm to include the clan of beauties.

Miss Silk looked Pepper up and down like she was a poor cut of meat. "So you're not one of us. I didn't think so."

Pepper wanted to kick Miss Silk in the shin, but smiled. "I'm here to do a story. I'm a reporter."

"Oh!" The woman turned toward the clucking mob. "Girls, they've sent a reporter. They're doing a story about us."

The women hovered around Pepper like kids promised free candy, all talking at once.

"Excuse me, one at a time," Pepper shouted above the din of excited females. Being near six feet in height, she garnered their attention and addressed herself to Miss Silk. "Can you tell me what brought you here tonight?"

As Miss Silk opened her mouth to answer, Mr. Nucretah's assistant clapped her bony hands. "Quiet, ladies. The Governor is ready to see you. And remember, only speak when asked."

Pepper's gaze flew to the model-skinny assistant. Raising her hand over the heads of the eager crowd, Pepper caught her attention. "They're getting in to see Mr. Nucretah?"

"Yes, yes. You all are. Line up and enter in an orderly fashion." The assistant moved to the office door. "He'll look you over and make his decision. Once he's voiced his preference, it's final. Those not chosen will leave quickly and quietly."

After waiting three nights in a stiff metal chair, Pepper wasn't about to miss her chance. She fell in line behind Miss Silk. Whatever they were vying for, Pepper intended to stick around long enough to ask Nucretah some questions. *I have to get to my dad and the Governor is the only man who can help. Nothing matters more. To hell with the story.*

The assistant herded them into the plush office. A hush fell on the group as they took in the splendor of thick Persian carpet, black leather chairs, and a sleek onyx desk where the most captivating man Pepper had ever seen, held court.

Rafe Nucretah scanned the line up and Pepper's mouth went dry. He was up to something. She felt it in her gut and she always trusted her intuition. Any man who looked that gorgeous had to be guilty of some crime. Being an alien vampire and a politician increased the likelihood.

He rose from his desk with the fluid grace of a predator

and stalked toward them. His chiseled features, sleek black hair, and dark brown eyes made it difficult to think. *Get a grip, girl.* He was only the most attractive man she'd ever seen, but her father's situation may be serious and she had to keep her head.

When his gaze rested on her, heat filled her cheeks and trickled down to her belly. She had to keep her wits. *Like me. Like me.* She ran the mantra through her mind and flashed her most charming smile. He raised an ebony brow, but showed no other interest.

"Turn, please," said the assistant.

They each made a slow rotation. It reminded Pepper of the, now-defunct, Westminster Dog Show. And she doubted she'd win "best of breed". *How humiliating.*

Once the line had completed its turn and again faced the Greek god, Pepper knew what he'd say a nanosecond before the words escaped his full lips.

"This one." He nodded at Pepper.

She jerked her head to stare at the man who'd chosen her over all the lovelies. Maybe he needed a secretary or some menial laborer. No chance he'd picked her over the ravishing girls to be an accessory at a state dinner. It didn't matter. She'd do anything if he'd help her father.

"The rest of you will now leave." The assistant held the door open. "The front desk will validate for parking."

Miss Silk sneered at Pepper as she glared through her lashes and flounced out with the rest of the grumbling pack. At this point, Pepper braced herself to lay her case at his feet. *I'll kiss his feet if it'll help.* The moist fingers of her left hand tightened on her computer, snugly tucked under her arm. Sweat dampened her skin wilting her blouse. Thank goodness her jacket hid her nerves. "Excuse me, Mr. Nucretah," she squeaked.

"Rafe." He smiled.

The simple act of twisting up the corners of his mouth made her legs wobble. *Here's your chance, say something.* But she couldn't get out another word.

"A car will be sent for you at six tomorrow evening. Give Celeste your address before you leave." He leaned against his desk and stared at her. There was something unusual about the look, as if he were trying to see through her, but couldn't.

"But I…" mumbled Pepper, as the assistant moved to her side and indicated the door. "No." Pepper's heart raced and she took a step toward the Governor. She couldn't lose her chance. "I need to talk to you."

"Very well. We may as well talk now. Celeste, leave us."

The assistant pursed her thin lips and left them alone. Anxiety tightened Pepper's chest as she heard the door click shut. She needed information about her father and Nucretah's help, if he'd give it. Everyone knew the aliens were stubborn, controlling, unfeeling warriors. Sympathy wouldn't move him. But they had a clan mentality, and they valued family. Her father was all she had. Pressing that point might work.

"Be seated." He gestured toward one of the tufted leather chairs opposite him as he claimed his seat behind the desk.

How honest should I be? The man wasn't one to be played with, and rumors persisted of the alien's ability to read minds. She perched on the edge of the chair and clutched her computer to her chest. *Better to come out with it.* "First things first. I'm afraid I'm here under false pretenses. I'm Pepper Morgan and I didn't come for this. I just had to get in to see you." Waves of his displeasure flowed across the stone desk, rattling her.

His mouth tightened. "You may not have intended to apply, but you've been chosen. My decision stands."

"What's the situation? Maybe we can work out a deal. You

give me the help I need and I run your errands or whatever for a few days."

"It's nothing like that."

"What is it, then? I'm a hard worker. I'll do about anything for your help. It's important to me."

He stood and his mouth twitched. "Glad to know you'll make an effort. I've claimed you as my mate."

Her stomach plummeted, her legs shook, and if she'd thought running was an option, she would have. Her computer slipped from her hands and fell to the floor with a thud. "What? You can't. I can't. We just met."

"The binding is tomorrow night." He didn't bother to look at her and spoke into the intercom. "Celeste, get someone to escort Pepper home and pack her things."

She jumped to her feet. "No!"

"Not an option." He spared her a glance as he shuffled through papers on his desk.

'I won't do it."

"You will."

She slammed her hand on the desk and winced from the force. "But I don't love you."

"That's not my concern." He retrieved a page from the

stack.

"It's not right. You can't mean to force me. There are laws protecting humans from Kivronaian abuse." She rubbed the tender flesh of her bruised palm with her fingers.

He lifted his focus to her. The power and authority in his gaze made her squirm. This man held the lives of thousands in his grasp and she knew it. So did he. "Do I have to remind you that in this sector, I am the law?"

Though his voice remained soft, the harsh reality of that statement she knew too well. He controlled everything, from granting permission to leave Red Rock, to the blood tax on humanity. And now, he had his sights on her. "Why not claim one of the other women? I'm sure any of them would be ecstatic."

"I don't want any of them. I want you."

"Why?"

"You're different."

She quelled the urge to scream, her body as tight as a bowstring. "That's not much of a reason to get married."

"More than enough of a reason." The pronouncement was barely above a whisper, but it carried a lethal edge concealed in his velvet voice. "You said you'd do anything for my help.

What do you want?"

"Want?"

"Yes. I tire of this argument and I've another meeting. Let's expedite this. We both know you must surrender."

She flinched. "You haven't given me much choice."

"None." He put down the paper and moved close enough that she could catch his spicy scent, a mix of cinnamon and something unrecognizable that made her mouth water. His dark gaze leveled on her face. "I'm not negotiating. But I am willing to grant you a favor, call it a wedding present."

She looked him in the eye, trying to seem braver than she felt. "Do I have your promise?"

"Everything I say is a promise."

The chance of seeing her father had dropped into her lap, but at a high price, marriage to a cold, bloodthirsty alien. Fear clutched her heart. *I can do this. I have to.* She trembled as she forced out the words. "I'll agree and not fight you, but I want my father brought home."

He cocked his head and raised a dark brow. "A small request. Very well. Done."

Pepper released the breath she hadn't realized she'd been holding. Relief washed over her frayed nerves and tears filled her eyes. "Thank you," she murmured, staring at the carpet.

"Where might I find your sire? Is he in another sector or continent?"

She lifted her head and blinked back the moistness. "Kivron. He was transferred six months ago."

Rafe didn't move, didn't drop eye contact, but a shadow crossed between them. "I'll look into it."

Darkness invaded her heart and she feared. *I'm never going to see my father again.* "You promised." Her voice quavered as her emotions spilled over in silent tears. She hated that he saw her vulnerable.

His brown eyes softened and he placed his large hands on her shoulders, firm, but gentle. "I..." he hesitated. "I will keep my word."

Termors ran through her body. His touch unnerved her. She needed to be held, needed strong arms to comfort her, a firm chest to lay her head upon, a safe place. She needed her father, not this stranger. Flashes of unknown need seared her, but they weren't hers. She shook her head, confused, and stepped back from his reach.

His mouth tightened, he put his hands behind his back, and stared ahead. "The binding will take place, make no mistake. There is no annulment and no divorce. It's eternal."

Her heart slammed against her ribs. "Eternal?"

"Due to the ritual's sacred nature, I can't explain what occurs. It's a simple ceremony. An appropriate gown will be provided."

"It's too fast." Panic raced through her veins. "Can't we wait a while?"

"To what purpose?"

"To get to know each other, of course." Her legs shook. She wiped her damp palms on the seams of her skirt.

"That's what the binding is for."

"You've got to be kidding."

He narrowed his eyes to hard, black slits of determination. "I assure you, I'm not."

CHAPTER TWO

With Pepper safely escorted home, Rafe sighed and ran a hand through his hair in frustration. Bad enough he couldn't bring her father back, he doubted anyone could manage that, but he'd promised. And now, he'd lied to her, saying he'd do all in his power to return her father to Earth just to ease her fears. *What's possessed me?*

He fell back into his chair, exasperated. It had to be the madness. It had taken over his mind and body, and made him say things that were out of character. He didn't allow himself to be affected like this. Her tears were none of his concern, but when she'd stared up at him, her big green eyes glistening, her voice choked with emotion, he couldn't stop himself from comforting her. *Silch.*

Insanity was to blame. Nothing else could account for his behavior or his inability to read her thoughts. He'd heard that it happened to every Kivronian on occasion, though never to him. Stepping into the minds of humans had always been as simple as breathing. The sudden dearth shook him. What the illness took, you didn't regain by binding alone. He grumbled a string of Kivronian oaths. He could control his response to fatigue and violent prodding, but to lose his most basic gifts. *Unacceptable.* Could the madness affect his abilities so quickly?

There had to be another explanation.

When the line of females had entered, he'd opened his mind as always to glean needed information. The silence that greeted his efforts to read Pepper's thoughts had worried him. He'd seriously considered insanity had tainted his gifts, but he'd heard the inane interior babbling of the other women easily enough. Each vacuous thought bombarded him, until Pepper.

He'd focused intently on her fragile beauty. A pleasant task. Her luminous eyes, full lips, and abundant auburn hair cascading in soft waves over her slender form were compelling diversions. And he looked forward to enjoying them fully on closer inspection.

It was the recognition he'd felt when he'd met her sparkling gaze. It held him. An odd reaction. *I've never experienced that before.* He'd liked her, and he hadn't counted on liking any of the women. They were a means to an end, something to check off from his list of duties to perform. Yet, when he'd looked on Pepper, he'd found her shabby attire refreshing. No expensive façade, no grasping for personal gain. The others had aspirations regarding him. It turned his stomach. Not Pepper. She could have asked for almost anything, but all she wanted was her father. He shook his head. *And I promised. I have lost my mind.*

If it wasn't madness affecting his abilities, the woman must be unusual. The idea held merit. Since he had to claim a human, Pepper might be the best option. The anomaly could be hers, a protection or biological difference. He smiled at his luck. If that proved out, he'd be relieved of ever having to wade through the illogical minefield between her lovely ears. In time, he'd learn what made her unique and solve the puzzle, but not tonight. Other matters required his attention.

His promise to Pepper must be addressed. He'd assign Dante reconnaissance on what became of her father. A man as valuable as Dr. Ben Morgan might be alive and transferred to Kivron. There was a slim chance and Rafe hoped that was the case. *I don't relish telling her otherwise.* If her father had been transferred, he was sorely needed on Kivron. It would take an executive order to get him home. Rafe didn't have the clout with the Supreme Commander to ask that favor.

A knock was heard at the door and Celeste entered. The

woman was no beauty, but she was Kivronian and that made her a prize. "The High Council will attend and I've seen to the caterer. What do you want me to tell the Council President about her background?"

Celeste had fussed at him when she realized he'd claimed a woman who had not been vetted by the registry. Though Pepper hadn't been screened with the rest of the greedy vipers, it didn't concern him. He respected her motives. He held family loyalty and love in high regard. They had that in common. What else did he need to know? "I'll take care of it." The President would be relieved Rafe would be taking a mate, one less insane Kivronian male to exterminate.

Celeste left and Rafe relaxed into the soft leather chair. Tomorrow night, he'd be bound. The threat of madness overcoming him diminished. Centuries ago, Hebric had saved his life in battle, and in his comrade's final moments, he'd done it again. A lump formed in Rafe's throat and he touched his red silk tie. *Thank you, my friend.*

# # #

Pepper had spent a fitful night. Armed Enforcers stood guard outside the little brick bungalow that she and her father called home. Their black forms, stalking past the windows cast shadows, making her uneasy.

It reminded her of the soldiers that had guarded her father as he worked on a cure for the plague. Even as a teen, she'd understood the need. Looting and murder had become the norm. Marauding bands had taken what they'd wanted and protection had been necessary — then.

She pulled back the pink, ruffled curtain from her bedroom window. A man encased in jet battle gear stared back at her, eyes dark and lethal. Rafe said protection was necessary for her safety, but she wasn't buying it. She felt like a prisoner. Did her father live under similar conditions? What incentive had they pressed upon him?

A shiver ran over her skin and she rubbed her arms to erase the gooseflesh. It wasn't cold, but she couldn't shake the chill in her blood. Packing her belongings had distracted her from thinking much about her future, choosing rather to focus on the task at hand, and the hope of seeing her father. At least, until one of the aliens gave her a fifteen-minute warning.

Almost six.

Where had the day gone? She shook her head. *That wasn't right. Where had her life gone?* Had she sold herself for a mess of pottage? If Rafe delivered her father, giving up her work and freedom would be worth it. *If.* He'd promised, but uneasiness sat in the back of her brain.

Since taking over, the aliens had promised many things. The plague had been eradicated, but that served them. The vampires needed a healthy human blood supply. They made sure there were plenty of nutritious food pellets for humans to eat, but what she wouldn't give for a burger, fries and a shake. Her mouth watered. *I haven't tasted chocolate since I was twelve.*

The aliens had promised to fill human needs as they helped rebuild society, and they had, in a fashion. Kivronians hadn't lied exactly, but they often bent the truth to their advantage.

Can I trust him?

Pepper mulled the question over in her mind, as she tucked her photo album into her carry-on, and swung the bag over her shoulder. Looking over the bedroom she'd had since childhood, she allowed the memories to fill her. The tattered quilt she and her mom had pieced together from scraps, her mother's wooden rocker where Pepper had made the decision to become a journalist, and the thrift-store dresser she'd refinished with her father, all held bits of a life shared with family she loved. And she was leaving it behind. The treasures she was allowed to take had to fit in her bag.

The steady ache in her chest spread to her stomach. *Nucretah promised.* But what's the word of an alien worth when given to a human? In her experience—little to none. Asking him to bring her father home had been courageous. Agreeing to the binding—desperate. Her father would call it foolish.

Pepper's eyes burned, but she refused to cry. She'd given her word to go through with the binding and Rafe had promised to find her father—finally. He didn't want to. She'd felt his hesitation. The vow had come hard, like a wary source weighing the choice to divulge the truth or not. Had he lied?

Pepper moved through the house holding objects, as if she could absorb the memories through her skin. Dealing with loss should come easy by now, it didn't. Each time, the weight threatened to crush her, but somehow she learned to let go and survive.

With a gentle hand, she stroked the maple grain of the kitchen table, moving to the scar caused by her father's coffee mug. Her finger traced the pale ring. Recalling the hours playing cards together until late at night, the laughter when she'd catch him cheating—badly. She smiled through the pain in her chest, opened the cupboard, pulled out the old blue mug and slipped it into her bag. Unshed tears clogged her throat.

She coughed, and adjusted the strap on her shoulder.

A new life lay ahead with a man she didn't know or understand. She'd make a go of it, as she did with everything she tackled. But for a bride-to-be, she felt no joy or lusty anticipation. *How sad is this?* Youthful dreams of romance, a big wedding with flowers, and an exotic honeymoon had gone up in smoke years ago. Victims of the plague and its aftermath, along with friends and the young man she'd loved. Tears blurred her vision. *Silly. I thought I was over that.* She blinked them away and focused on Rafe.

The man was a force of nature, but also surprisingly gentle. She wouldn't have guessed that. When she'd humiliated herself by asking for reassurance, he'd held her, stroked her hair and whispered his promise. For a man with a reputation as a ruthless, cold-hearted, self-serving politician, he had another side, and she liked that other part of him. If it had been merely an act or he'd been lying, she would've known. *But he's an alien. Does my intuition work with him?*

"Five minutes," called one of the Enforcers.

Fear constricted her throat. Her breath came in gasps. *It's okay. I'm going to be fine.* She silently repeated the words as she willed her feet toward the front door. Tonight she'd be married to a stranger, a man who existed on human blood. Visions of Scheherazade's weaving of tales to entice her murderous husband into allowing her live one more night haunted her. Pepper squelched the panic that had moved to her legs making them quiver. When Rafe tired of her, what inducement could she offer him? *One thousand and one stories wouldn't cut it.*

"It's time." An Enforcer stood in the doorway like a demon welcoming her to Hell. Pepper sucked in a breath and pushed her unwilling body onto the porch.

She was being ridiculous. Nothing in Rafe's manner toward her indicated violence. There was a time last year, when he'd sliced an opponent in two with one blow, but that was in battle. Their relationship wouldn't be adversarial. *I hope not.* But which was the real Rafe, the man who'd held her tenderly or the vicious warrior?

# # #

Bound. Rafe strode through the Great Hall of the High Council forcing himself to care about such mundane things as table linens and decorations, when all that interested him was an end to the fatigue and vile whispers from the madness attacking his mind.

Would the ceremony bring relief or just curb the insanity's

progress? Warriors who had waited to claim a mate until insanity had grown obvious would never admit the true state of their condition.

Show no weakness, first of the Kivronian dictates.

The axiom emblazoned Rafe's family banner. All warriors carried similar sentiments into battle. *Defend or die*, had been Hebric's. Rafe rubbed his stinging eyes with his fingers. *I'm in control.*

Rafe had a reputation to uphold, tonight, more than ever. A high-level dignitary would be in attendance and Rafe's public persona must be impeccable. Strong, ambitious, and ruthless, that's what he was known for being. The image must be maintained.

The role he'd created served his purposes. A man solely focused on political advancement, superficial, loyal to whichever cause benefited him most. No one expected him to stand for high ideals like honor or justice, and he needed that to continue, but he'd played the part so long. His jaw tightened. Had it changed him?

Clicking heals stole his attention and Rafe turned to see Celeste's skinny form hurrying to his side. "Mr. Nucretah." She smiled and handed him a glass of blood. "Taste it. The caterer wants your opinion."

Taking the glass, he brought it to his lips and enjoyed the fragrance. Though the High Council had ruled it illegal to partake directly from humans, they still appreciated an excellent source served at 98.6 degrees. He sipped and let the liquid flow over his tongue, the flavor, unmistakable: the rich, healthy blood of humans in their prime. Setting up blood-draw stations on college and high school campuses to pay the blood tax had been his brilliant idea. Those Kivronians with resources gladly paid the increased price. Rafe drained his glass. The extra funds helped him with his other pursuits. "The dignitary will be impressed."

"Who is it?" Celeste tilted her head, her black hair swinging over her thin shoulders.

"I haven't been able to find out. No one is supposed to know he's coming."

Her silver eyes glowed in the dim light giving her the appearance of a hungry feline. "A surprise visit. Interesting."

"Yes."

Celeste took his glass. "I'll let the caterer know you approve." She left in a billow of white fabric.

Rafe tugged on the sleeves of his charcoal gray, dress

uniform. The black tie at his neck felt constrictive, so he loosened it. Surprise visits from the elite were uncommon. They usually occurred for one of two reasons, either you were being singled out for advancement, or there was a threat in the sector. It wasn't a promotion.

Problems existed with human rebels, but the Western Quadrant was no different from any other in that regard. The Council wanted rebellion contained. Easier said than done. The nameless rabble hid and lashed out periodically with thefts from the blood depository, but nothing to gain the notice of a high-ranking official. There was no point in thinking more about the visit, not in his current state of mental fog. He'd find out soon enough.

Better to focus on the public festivities ahead. The binding would begin his and Pepper's thirty nights of courtship, a betrothal in human terms. Completely binding them for eternity, but not by flesh. For that he'd be forced to wait. *Thirty long nights.* How could a man be expected to bear it? To have the woman under his roof, near enough to touch, kiss, hold, but forbidden to take all he wanted. He shook his head. To remain celibate for so long. He hadn't denied himself the pleasures of a woman's body for more than a week in centuries.

Duty, tradition, and family honor demanded he hold to the course and prevail against his own desires. He could indulge in affection toward her, but not consummate it. Falling to passion before completion of betrothal would be a monstrous mistake. He'd be cursed with insanity for eternity, but Pepper would be condemned to madness within hours of enjoying each other. His jaw clenched. Few humans lasted a week listening to desire's evil breathings, before taking their lives. *I'm in control. It won't touch her.* He was a warrior, used to denying himself in the field, trained to focus on a task and eschew his body's urgings. He could check his needs. But her soft skin, the way her lips curved in invitation. *Silch. I want her all ready.*

The thought of Pepper in his arms warmed him, as much as it concerned him. Her arguing with him made him smile. Few warriors had the courage to oppose him, but she'd forcefully refused his claim. *Refused.* No cowering to beg for mercy, although that any human female would spurn him was unimaginable. He shrugged.

She valued being in love. So did he, but for different reasons. He needed her devotion. Only with it, would the transference of blood heal the remainder of the madness rampaging within him. Binding her was his first target, next her acceptance. Love would undoubtedly follow.

Too many females to count had sworn their love to him, but they'd lied. He shook his head in disgust. Their thoughts had betrayed their motives. Many had wanted wealth, others importance. All desired something from their connection to him, but none had bothered to look beyond his appearance and position to Rafe, the man.

Pepper was different. She used her intellect rather than her body to negotiate, and what she wanted didn't involve tying herself to him. That had been his idea. He smiled. Though the bulky jacket she'd worn did nothing to enhance her charms, he could see she had long shapely legs, and the slim skirt made the most of her well-formed backside. He licked his lips in anticipation. Duty and survival weren't the only things spurring him on.

As a warrior, he enjoyed the hunt. Pepper was a challenge. Her sharp edges and fortified exterior collided with the soft, emotional nature lurking beneath her surface. He had every intention of breaking down her defenses. Even a woman as hesitant and tightly wound as Miss Morgan couldn't long withstand his considerable talents of persuasion. Once he conquered her reserve, it would be a simple thing to secure her most tender feelings.

# # #

She paced the room like a caged animal. And wasn't that the truth? Pepper stopped to glare at her reflection in the golden baroque mirror. This had once been Red Rock's finest hotel. Now it belonged to the Kivronian High Council. They had commandeered everything of value. The chandelier above her head dripped with crystal. The beige carpet was so thick she could barely distinguish her bare toes through its pile. Her gaze shifted to the silk dress clinging to her curves. *Black. How appropriate.*

Rafe had claimed her—fine. But why be bound so soon? She ran her fingers through her mass of auburn hair, having given up the attempt to put it up. Impossible. Her hair billowed around her face and shoulders like a cloud. Not attractive. She scowled and tried for a French braid.

As she plaited the long reddish strands, her mind sought to weave sense of Rafe's claim. Why? Her journalistic instincts couldn't let it go, and that meant there was a story, not that she'd be allowed to write it. Something didn't feel right.

She'd been so focused on her father that the utter strangeness of her situation hadn't occurred to her at the time.

The most eligible Kivronian bachelor in the Western Hemisphere had claimed a woman he knew nothing about. And while she wasn't a complete toad, she wasn't a stunning beauty, either. It couldn't be about sex. What was he up to?

His actions seemed desperate, as if he had to bind a woman, any woman, and do it now. That was the bones of it. But how could claiming her be of use to him?

She was nobody.

An awful possibility hit her between the eyes. *Maybe that was the point. As humans went, I'm expendable.* Did he claim her because it wouldn't matter if something happened to her? The idea twisted her stomach.

The aliens shared little of their culture and less of their rituals. She had no idea what would occur tonight. The binding might entail anything. All Rafe had been willing to say was their marriage would last forever. A surge of panic quickened her pulse. Pepper steadied herself against the bathroom sink and noticed her handiwork. She grimaced at the threads of hair sticking out from the braid and pulled it loose. "Ugh!"

Kivronians had no reservations about sex with humans, but few aliens had taken them as mates. Why? What if the ritual were dangerous? What if the chances of a human living through it were slight? Pepper wrapped her arms tight around her waist. Under those circumstances, she could see the wisdom in not being emotionally attached. Pepper breathed through the rising nausea. Rafe didn't know her, so of course she didn't matter to him. *What have I gotten myself into?*

Her fingers skimmed the sleek black silk. Not what she'd envisioned in her childhood dreams of walking down the isle. The gown was long and hugged her body, too tight for her taste. She looked as if she'd been poured into it. Pepper crinkled her nose at her reflection. The dress was too sexy, too revealing with its open back and bared shoulders. *I can't get away with this. I'm not sophisticated.* The gown was elegant and she felt ridiculous.

Pepper dampened her hands in the sink, and patted her unruly strands to calm them, but to little effect. Her hair looked as out of control as she felt. Nothing explained Rafe's urgency. The entire claim made no sense. A man like Rafe calculated everything. Nothing was left to chance, certainly not something as important as marriage. There were reasons for his actions, she just didn't know them yet.

A good reporter excelled at gathering facts. And she was a good reporter. If Rafe wouldn't tell her his reasons, then she'd find the truth another way. Her instinct about him had to be right. Rafe Nucretah was up to something.

She gave up on her hair and padded to the bed, a huge, ornately carved canopy ensconced in rose and gold brocade. Not her style. She preferred simple, clean lines. *I'm as out of place in this room as I am with Rafe.*

The mattress dipped as she lowered herself onto the edge. As tempting as Rafe was, she had no intention of consummating anything. Going through with the binding because she'd given her word, and she'd had little choice, was one thing. But intimacy with a man she didn't know, was quite another. She'd never been that kind of girl. Rafe may have other ideas, but on that she'd stand firm. Pepper needed a deep connection before she could give herself to any man.

Uncertainty had been the underlying current of her life. Forced to survive by protecting her heart, doling out her trust bit by bit, she'd learned to rely on her intuition. Now she trusted her gut before her eyes. The words of some demanding politician wouldn't sway her. Her senses warned to be cautious.

Rafe was obviously using her for some hidden purpose. Since she'd been coerced into the situation, she'd take up the game, but not as a defenseless pawn. She'd relentlessly use her skills to uncover the real reason for his claim, and once she knew the truth, she would renegotiate her terms.

CHAPTER THREE

A room had been dedicated for Kivronian rites. Stripped of human adornments, the paintings had been replaced with landscapes of Kivron, jagged rock reaching up against a dusky sky, two moons illuminating the scene below. Rafe missed his planet, but things had changed since their civil war. Earth was home now.

He focused on the ebony table in the center of the rectangular room. A piece of the sacred Talas stone, the size of his fist, shone blacker than the table it sat upon. Black symbolized all that was best in Kivronian culture, the three virtues of honor, truth, and strength. Those sentiments would be part of tonight's binding, a promise made between him and Pepper, together with Kivronian society. Vows made here were eternal. Breaking them carried severe penalty.

The carpet had been removed in favor of black marble. The white walls, the color of loyalty. Rafe shook his head and smiled. Celeste's flowing white gown had been her choice, a sign of respect to him, though unbecoming against her chalky skin. A nice gesture on her part.

He paced the room waiting for Pepper. No one had arrived yet. Preferring solitude and the sound of his leather shoes scuffing the floor to the madness whispering in his head, Rafe utilized the quiet to gain control of his mind. Even prior to the insanity he had demanded control of things around him. It had worked when he'd served as general in the Kivronian military, but it taxed him on Earth. His shoulders tightened. Humans didn't understand order or his demand for it.

This room's singular design and purpose were to act as a haven against human chaos. The only furnishings were the table displaying the stone and an ebony cabinet stark against the wall. He studied the dark chest. It contained sacred ritual implements, such as the *Dagger of Embri*. Tension crept up his neck. Humans were skittish creatures and he hoped Pepper didn't scream when she saw the knife.

The door opened, and everything receded into the background, as Rafe viewed his bride escorted by Celeste. The two couldn't be more different. Pepper's tall form, auburn hair, and soft, warm skin made Celeste's slight body and pale flesh look dead. *Unfortunate female.* She'd make some Kivronian male a good mate, but he was relieved she wouldn't fall to him. Children or not, eternity was a very long time.

He scanned Pepper, relishing how the gown accentuated her charms. No one would've guessed voluptuous curves had existed beneath her worn suit. *Breathtaking.* He'd thought the girl would be an enjoyable duty, but with Pepper's treasures more openly displayed, she tempted him. The fall of her hair suggested wild sensuality. Her parted lips invited fantasies of what he'd do with that mouth at completion of their betrothal. That night promised a feast of pleasure. He licked his lips, the tips of his fangs erupting in his mouth as desire flicked low. He willed them back. *No need to frighten her.*

Madness goaded him to take her hard and fast once given opportunity, but Pepper's life demanded he wait. Satisfying his lust showed weakness. He was strong and in control. Both the whispers and his need must be ignored, his energy focused in other directions like securing Pepper's love. How might he accomplish that?

If he'd chosen one of the other women begging for his attention, he might fail to gain love and the full cure to the madness riding him even now. Such females wouldn't do. Those mercenary women were impervious to tender emotion. He'd be doomed to suffer forever bound to any of them. Pepper possessed the caring nature capable of saving him. She just needed coaxing.

A strand of her hair fell across her face. He reached up to place it behind her ear and his fingers brushed the slender column of her neck. She froze beneath his touch. Her eyes darted toward his face with the wariness of a cornered animal. She feared him.

Silch. That wouldn't do. He usually preferred a degree of dread in humans. It kept them in line, compliant to his demands, but not now. Misgivings would hinder any affection for him. Gaining her trust would take time and effort. It was the time that annoyed him, not the effort. He didn't have it. Based on his sense of her, it might take weeks to dismantle her anxiety, longer to win her heart.

"I must."

Insanity had fouled both his energy and his mental acuity. He had no clear promise that binding would restore either, just the hope. With Pepper living with him, he'd struggle constantly to hide the signs of his illness. No time to relax if fatigue left him prostrate, no understanding for his short temper if voices urged violence. *No escape.* He couldn't tell her of the madness threatening them all, that her love alone could cure what raged in his mind. He didn't need kindness or sympathy. He needed her tenderness, passion, her desire to care for him beyond his imperfection, and to love him.

At month's end, if he hadn't succeeded in securing her love, then the insanity would ignite and explode making Hebric's massacre of eighteen people, merely a belch. Rafe shuddered. The volcanic force of his madness would be uncontrollable. He would become a monster with strength and cunning, his skills augmented to that of a god, an evil creature devastating all within his reach. He trembled, knowing what he must do, and stilled his body. *I'm in control, for now.* He'd have to talk to his brothers before long, and attain their oath to exterminate him, should it come to that.

Rafe pulled himself away from shadows of destruction and focused on solving the problem. How to court a woman like Pepper? He'd have to do all in his power to capture her heart. Seduction and plying with gifts, that's what the rest of the female population wanted from him. Rafe surveyed the wide-eyed innocence of her face. Pepper wasn't like the rest. Their conversation had shown she had integrity and a willingness to sacrifice for others. He respected her for it, but it posed a problem. She couldn't be bought or easily won.

Rafe reached out to her, his hand an invitation and a test of her trust. Would she take it? She stared at his hand, her lovely mouth pursed, and then she wrapped her slender arms over her waist. A dull ache filled his chest. No woman had *ever* refused him. He was determined to conquer by whatever means necessary.

# # #

Pepper entered with Celeste and surveyed the lifeless room. It lacked any hint of color or celebration. *This is my wedding, the only one I'll ever have. I want to cry.*

Rafe stood near the table and looked up. At least, he didn't appear displeased. This binding served a purpose for him beyond claiming a mate, and she was adequate or he wouldn't have picked her. What were his reasons?

Pepper watched Celeste as she glided past, her white toga skimming her figure like butterfly wings. The vampire reminded Pepper of an ancient goddess, classic features surrounded by sleek blue-black hair, swinging over her shoulders. No one would ever call Pepper classic. She pushed her unruly auburn waves from her face. Pepper knew her strengths, but refined and alluring weren't among them.

With the fluid motion of a predator, Rafe moved in front of her. His stare made her shiver. Pepper knew that look, determined hunger refusing to be denied. Most women crumbled at his heated gaze. His sophistication made their knees weak, but none of that mattered. No amount of blatant, sexual appeal could convince her to sleep with him. A relationship built on trust and mutual respect had to be in place first. She chewed at her bottom lip. Would he accept her terms? Doubtful. With his reputation, he took what he wanted, like all vampires. They didn't ask. She was lucky he'd accommodated her request for her father.

He licked his lips and she glimpsed the tips of white fangs. He reminded her of a panther on the hunt. Kivronians lived on human blood and at that moment, she felt like dinner. Were her fears justified? Maybe not, but she had them. Her legs shook under the long, black gown. It rustled. Pepper locked her knees to stop the movement and hoped she wouldn't faint.

Rafe leaned closer, breathed in, and then touched her neck. He lingered and caressed. She couldn't move, a deer caught in headlights. Her heart beat out a rapid tattoo. Her mind flew to old vampire movies and bites to vulnerable flesh. Did the ritual include blood?

Stop it. Those stories were only loosely derived from Kivronians. The aliens were civilized. She took a deep breath to calm herself, and with it came two words into her head: *control, conquer*. That worried her. Not good words if they came from her soon-to-be husband. She had no intention of being controlled, much less conquered. *Silly*. She didn't read minds. A little intuition, but she wasn't psychic. *It's nerves.* She ventured a glance at his handsome face. His expression gave nothing away.

When he lifted his hand, palm up, beckoning to her, she noticed the tips of sharp, retractable claws. Of course, she'd seen them before, but had no intimate knowledge. Vampires were designed to kill. Everything about them was both compelling and lethal. She swallowed the lump in her throat and hugged her arms tighter around her body.

Pepper knew she should've accepted his hand, but couldn't. His eyes had taken on a disappointed cast. *He couldn't care. Not about me.* He was using her for some purpose and that's all. She needed to remember that. The softness in his eyes had to be a trick of the light.

"The dress suits you." Rafe smiled, his fangs gone, and Pepper breathed a sigh of relief. "You're nervous. Let me put you at ease." He stepped back. "Better?"

She wouldn't openly admit it, but when he'd moved away,

she wished he hadn't. *It's their natural magnetism. It's not honest attraction. It's not real.* "I'm getting bound. Every bride is nervous."

"Of course." The corner of his mouth twitched.

A procession of aliens draped in black robes entered. Hoods concealed their identities, making them as hidden from her as the ritual. Looking like specters of the Grim Reaper, preparing to mow down life, their stiff carriage gave the impression of a funeral rather than a wedding.

In some ways, it was a funeral. Pepper would be ostracized, not fully accepted by Kivronians and shunned by humans. Most people feared and distrusted the vampires. A human who joined the invaders might be politely tolerated in public, but privately viewed as a traitor. Her friends would be *busy* when she called. Until Rafe returned her father, she'd be alone, suspended between two worlds. Her stomach twisted. Humans weren't allowed to view the ritual, so no friend stood with her at her wedding. She might as well get used to being an outcast.

She scanned the robed six and Celeste. Only Rafe acknowledged her as he slipped his arm around her waist and escorted her to the far end of the table. Her emotions jumbled as thoughts and feelings pressed in, fear, anxiety, then temptation and longing. Did she want him or was something else happening? Her intuition couldn't be picking up feelings from a vampire. *That's impossible.*

All stood silent and still as if waiting. A seven-foot-tall vampire strode in, barrel-chested, flowing red hair, and fierce, amber eyes. He wore a gray uniform similar to Rafe's. The giant leveled his gaze on the two of them. Rafe dug his fingers into Pepper's side, causing her to wince.

He immediately loosened his grip. "Lord Garmood Loth."

"Nucretah," grumbled the giant. "We shall begin."

Pepper didn't understand Kivronian. As each of the six spoke, Rafe nudged her, and she nodded at the appropriate time. Her attention wandered to Garmood. His face seemed familiar. Had he haunted a dream or had she seen him before?

Garmood studied her with precision, his cold stare was calculating. Her gut shrieked "danger", but there was no place to run. He nodded to her almost imperceptibly. He knew her or thought he did. Who was he and where had she seen him?

Whether a flash of intuition or a recurrence of memory, it didn't matter. Visions from the past slammed into her. Garmood had spoken with her father. It came in torrents, flooding into her mind. Her gut confirmed the dark, oily feel clinging to the disjointed memories. This was very bad.

# # #

Anger coursed through Rafe. He clenched his fists. Under different circumstances they'd battle, and Rafe would sever Garmood's head from his thick neck. Rafe's jaw tightened until he thought his teeth would crack. He wasn't at his best. The madness had affected him. Better to engage the *crimwad* when in full possession of his abilities. To say they hated each other didn't begin to describe Rafe's seething rage. His body vibrated with it. He squelched the insane whispers pushing him to leap over the table to rip Garmood's heart from his chest. *Not now.* An opportunity would surely come.

Garmood Loth had risen in leadership with the occurrence of a few untimely deaths. It didn't surprise Rafe. His enemy had powerful allies who wielded great authority. But why was he there? Earth wasn't the most desirable post. He certainly wasn't there to promote Rafe. Garmood attended the binding to unnerve him, perhaps see if Garmood could detect madness, and then order dissolution. Too late. The ritual was under way, insuring Rafe's survival. No one on the Supreme High Council could stop it.

Overcoming his enemy required a cool head and excellent strategy. Rafe needed information. Kivron didn't send officials on a whim. Garmood would be under command to accomplish something of importance. What was it? Dante could sniff out intelligence using his contacts, giving Rafe a chance to prepare. He needed an edge. The time had come to defeat the man who'd murdered Rafe's sisters.

Celeste chanted a ritual blessing, drawing Rafe's attention. She opened the cabinet, removed the Dagger of Embri and presented the eight-inch-long knife to Garmood. It disgusted Rafe that his enemy would seal the binding. He watched Pepper's eyes widen as Garmood chanted and raised the dagger, turning it in a circular motion. The overhead light caught the edge of the shiny blade. Anxiety oozed from Pepper. Rafe smelled it, so did Garmood, evident in the wicked gleam in his eyes.

Rafe held her close, wanting to comfort her rising dismay, concerned her anxiety over the ritual might push her further from him. Garmood returned the dagger to Celeste, who placed it on the table before Pepper. Her face went pale. Rafe tightened his grip on her waist.

"Pick up the dagger," Garmood instructed her, "and pierce

the tip of your left thumb."

Pepper's gaze of desperation and pleading flew to Rafe. There was nothing he could do, but nod encouragement. Her shoulders sagged in resignation. With quivering hands, she slit the end of her thumb. Blood dripped from the cut onto the table. Celeste dipped her fingers into the drops and applied them to the sacred stone.

"Smear your bloody thumb on Nucretah's mouth," said Garmood.

Pepper shook, but did as commanded. Pride for her courage swelled in Rafe. He accepted her offering and licked her blood from his lips. *Delicious.* He wondered if the rest of her tasted as sweet. That would have to wait until after the betrothal. Removing his arm from her, he retrieved a strip of black cloth from his jacket pocket and tied it over her wound.

She teetered, leaning against the table when he grasped the knife. Her dress rustled dispersing the pungent odor of fear. Rafe hoped she'd get through the ritual. He sliced his thumb and swathed the crimson fluid over her mouth. Pepper closed her eyes.

"Consume it," ordered Garmood.

Her eyes pinched shut and her mouth twisted, but her

tongue obediently slid over her full lips.

Rafe wanted to kiss her. She'd accepted the binding. The room filled with celebratory hisses, while Pepper coughed. She swayed. Rafe reached out to steady her and met her glistening stare. It began slowly, a spark igniting deep within him sending bright embers into his mind, each point of light diffusing shadows of insanity. Would the effect spread? He hoped so.

Strength trickled down his spine and seeped into his bones. He'd forgotten that force of power. It spilled into his flesh. He reveled in heat and vibrant energy, invincible against all foes. He glared at Garmood in warning. His enemy smiled.

Pepper had restored him in part. There remained some impairment, but he was most improved. Elated at the change and surging with amorous need, Rafe took Pepper in his arms and claimed her mouth with a kiss, as demanding and intense as the fire burning through him. He wanted her. Not just her mouth, with her flesh wrapped tight around him, but all of her, body and soul. *Mine.*

# # #

The coppery taste of blood coupled with Rafe's enticing essence. Pepper struggled with no success against the hard wall of his chest and the vice-like grip of his arms. His kiss deepened and her body relaxed. Warmth spread low in her belly. She cursed her body's response even as her mouth opened to his invasion. His tongue stroked, teased, and forced surrender. Pepper lost her battle in his torrid kiss.

When he released her throbbing lips, she staggered, and he tightened his hold on her. It didn't help. The taste of his mouth and feel of his hands on her were intoxicating. How could she fight against such force? She should try, at least until she uncovered Rafe's purpose in claiming her. But did she have the strength to deny her loneliness and the needy ache pulsing in her core? She breathed in his spicy scent that added to her stupor, but reality lurked behind Rafe in the form of Garmood, and it sobered her. His frigid glare chilled her to her bones.

Her father had never mentioned the oversized alien or the conversation she'd happened upon in his office five years ago. From the bits she'd heard, Garmood wanted something and her father had refused him. Pepper's pulse quickened at the memory of the vampire's bared fangs. She'd watched through a crack in the door. When the alien had moved to leave, she'd scurried into the refuge of the hall closet, cowering among the brooms and cleaning supplies. She'd never asked her father about Garmood, but now she wished she had.

"There's something unusual about your bride, Nucretah."

The muscles in Rafe's jaw worked and he turned around. "She's human, Lord Garmood. Pepper is unusual in many ways."

Garmood's amber eyes threatened. "I refer to something in particular."

Pepper's gut twisted. Warnings surged through her skin, leaving goosebumps. The two men reminded her of dogs fighting over a bone.

Sharp points of Rafe's fangs accompanied his answer. "And what might that be?"

Garmood made a show of his own impressive canines in a yawn. "Really Nucretah, stop this charade. You know perfectly well she's a black hole."

A low rumble vibrated Rafe's chest. The binding ritual had unnerved Pepper, and she still reeled from Rafe's kiss. Now she was being told she was a black hole. She knew the scientific explanation, but what did it mean in reference to her? She pasted on a smile as her knees quaked. "Excuse me, Lord Garmood. Why am I a black hole?"

Rafe clasped her hand and squeezed. His eyes held caution,

but no one needed to tell her to be wary of Garmood. The man's mere presence was enough, but the memory of that vampire's threatening of her father set every instinct on alert.

"Nucretah, you should keep your mate better informed," he reprimanded, and turned his attention to her, his gaze shifting from cold to welcoming. "A black hole, my dear, is someone whose mind registers as void. We can't read it. More than a closed door, which might be opened. You're emptiness. Perhaps a receiver of energy, while showing up blank."

Her pulse quickened. They couldn't read her thoughts, good news. But she did receive, had been picking up odd visions and ideas not her own. If the aliens knew she had any ability to delve through their thoughts, she'd be dead before her next breath. After all, she was human and nothing to the aliens. Other than Rafe, the rest had ignored her. Now, with Garmood's interest, every eye stared in speculation. Celeste's cold, silver gaze contained something else, anger or perhaps jealousy.

"Lord Garmood," said Rafe, in a clear baritone. "Enough physics lesson for now. Our guests are waiting. Would you present us to them? The festivities can't begin until we appear."

All heads swiveled to Garmood. Pepper didn't understand

much about Kivronian politics or their displays of power, but this looked like a stare down. Male supremacy exhibited with a challenge in every glare and turn of phrase. For some reason, she seemed to be the cause.

Garmood lowered his thick, red brows. He didn't move his gaze from Rafe for a protracted minute. She held her breath and noticed a bead of sweat trickle down the side of Rafe's neck. Nothing showed on his face, but her hand felt moist in his grasp.

If the two warriors insisted on playing chicken, she didn't want to stand too close. Rafe tightened his grip. Her fingers turned white and she wiggled them, but he didn't let up. The tension in his muscles thrummed. Pepper felt rage, anxiety, and determination pulse from his hand to hers. The mixture of feelings had to belong to Rafe. Her only emotion was simple fear.

For another agonizing moment, Garmood stood firm, a mass of muscle and confidence. She took a sideways glance at Rafe, handsome, strong, and capable, but he lacked surety. Why? A word sunk into her brain, *impaired*. Pepper shook her head in denial. *That can't be right.* She was the only impaired person in the room. If she were psychic, her gifts were unreliable.

Pepper couldn't take any more of this game. "Lord Garmood," she squeaked. "Please, do me the great honor of presenting us." She took a cautious step still tethered to Rafe.

Celeste gasped, one of the robed vampires coughed, and Pepper realized she'd made a social gaffe. She forged ahead. "I would be most grateful." She flashed a charming smile. Rafe yanked her back and secured her to his side. His entire body was so tight she thought he'd snap.

Garmood furrowed his wide brow. A hush fell over the room as all awaited his answer.

CHAPTER FOUR

Garmood opened his wide mouth and laughed, a rusty sound like old hinges. "I accept." The tension in the room dissipated. Except for Rafe's.

Position required Rafe to ask Garmood's favor, but Pepper batted her eyes, smiled, and flirtted with that monster. *Unacceptable.* She belonged to him. Rafe ached to remove Garmood's grin with the aid of his claws. A fight was what his enemy wanted, pushing Rafe to assault him in public, but waiting would give Rafe the advantage of surprise, a far superior position, and no witnesses. Swallowing the growl choking his throat, Rafe bowed to his enemy. "I am honored." The words tasted bitter and he wanted to spit.

Garmood was evil incarnate, devoid of loyalty to any cause, except his revenge against the Nucretah family. Rafe's sire had incurred his wrath millennia ago. In retaliation, Garmood had sworn to exterminate the entire clan, and thus far, he'd accomplished much. After Rafe's mother's death, the monster unleashed the full force of his venom, relentlessly murdering any unlucky enough to bear the name, Nucretah.

Anger seethed below Rafe's surface. He couldn't allow his bubbling fury to spill over onto Garmood, though he relished the chance to dispatch the villain. *Once I'm whole.* Let the monster think his skill might be compromised by madness. Garmood might get lax and give Rafe the opening he needed to end the senseless killing. His enemy had never tasted insanity, having been bound young and well loved. Rafe's lip curled. It sickened him to think his mother had once been joined to that creature. At least, she hadn't lived to see him butcher her daughters.

"Miss Morgan." Garmood slid his gaze to Rafe. "Forgive me, it's Nucretah now." His enemy spoke kindly, but Rafe saw the bait being laid for him. He wouldn't bite. "Let me guide you, my dear." Garmood smiled, looking as harmless as a sleeping cobra.

Pepper rustled toward the monster and placed her hand on his proffered arm. Her willingness to comply to such a creature's request, while denying his own, irked Rafe. Was she so lacking in judgment that she trusted this snake over him? *Patience.* She was human and knew nothing of Garmood or his history. Undoubtedly, she deferred to the wishes of an important official and nothing more.

Innocent human. She didn't realize the man would slice her throat just to spite Rafe. Garmood's position would shield him as he lied, claiming her a spy or some other ludicrous charge to justify killing her. Pepper was no more capable of subterfuge than Garmood was of mercy. The girl was too trusting. And that would make protecting her difficult. *I'll have to be vigilant.*

"Shall we?" Garmood grinned at Pepper and patted her hand, a kind gesture from someone else, but from this creature, a lure to catch prey. "You're charming. Nucretah has secured a gem. I'm surprised he had enough sense to recognize it."

Rafe bristled with anxiety for Pepper's safety. Did the monster mean to take her from him? Under certain conditions, it was possible. It's how Rafe's sire had secured their mother from Garmood. Rafe swore profusely in his mind. Of course, that could be his plan, to take his revenge in kind for his loss.

Why hadn't I realized?

This move of Garmood's, so blatant, so very much like him, Rafe should have seen it. Did insanity continue to cloud his thinking? No. It wasn't the remnants of madness alone. He berated himself for allowing anger to get in the way of his judgment. With such a cunning enemy, he shouldn't act without careful planning. But he must do something. Garmood would manipulate Pepper, gain advantage and then press his rights in open challenge against Rafe. No matter what, Rafe couldn't allow that to happen. He had to protect her.

# # #

He smelled of lemons, and the aroma reminded Pepper of the furniture polish her mother had used before everything crumbled. The scent gave her a warm cozy feel that argued with Garmood's dangerous appearance. Dressed in his gray uniform, rather than a battle suit, didn't make him any less fierce. Her impression could have to do with the first time she'd seen him as she lurked behind the door. Garmood had worn battle gear, his red hair tied back. She'd viewed him from the side as he'd sat at a table conversing with her father. Until now, she'd been unaware of the vampire's impressive height. Rafe stood only a few inches shorter, and was more lethal than most, but Garmood hummed with the ferocity of a wild animal.

He reminded her of a tiger lolling by a pool, passive until he scented prey. A chill ran over her. Was she his target or had he set his sights on Rafe? They obviously knew each other. What ever their past, the tension between them was so thick it was difficult to breathe. Resting her hand on Garmood's arm had taken courage. At any moment, she half expected him to level his yellow gaze on her and growl. Rafe stood behind them. She felt safer knowing he was there. Though she couldn't think what she'd do if this frightening, hulk of a man cornered her in a secluded room.

As they made their way to the elevator, Pepper tried to imagine why the alien dignitary paid her any deference. Her gut churned. Did he have news of her father? The two men knew each other. Hope took root in her chest and tightened her throat. Maybe her father had worked out an agreement with him. A powerful man like Garmood would be in a good position to bring her father home, but he'd ask something for the favor. The vampires did nothing without payment.

Pepper glanced up at the burley alien. Garmood was attractive, if a girl went for the merciless and imperious type. He stood erect, fit, and had strong masculine features. Though his mouth was well formed, the corners dipped down, making it appear hard rather than firm. The man had everything, position, and power. That's what mattered most to Kivronians. She couldn't fathom what had marred his life and left him bitter.

The elevator was a typical small box with gold foil paper lining the walls. Its occupants were unique, a copper-haired behemoth, a darkly sophisticated politician, and Pepper, sweating between the silent pair, praying for the elevator doors to open.

When the elevator stopped on the top floor, she couldn't escape the confined space fast enough. Garmood ended her flight, wrapping her arm around his and pinning her close. She struggled to keep up with his long strides down the hall to what had once been the grand ballroom. Based on the décor of the binding chamber, and the joyless ceremony, Pepper braced herself for further disappointment.

Garmood stopped at the gold inlaid doors. "Nucretah."

Pepper thought she'd heard Rafe say something under his breath, but he complied and opened the door for them, holding it as Garmood ducked to clear the frame.

Pepper blinked. It was exactly as she'd remembered it as a little girl. Her aunt's wedding reception had taken place here. The ornate moldings, picture windows overlooking the city, and intricate painted ceiling accented with gold made it look like a palace. Thick, wool carpet in an antique floral pattern graced the floor and gave way to an area for dancing. Round tables set with gold brocade linens, pale Kivronian flowers, and black tapers that flickered with light as it danced over crystal.

A buffet stretching along one wall smelled promising. A tower of fresh strawberries, warming trays, and the delectable aromas of five-star-cuisine awaited. Pepper's mouth watered. She didn't think she'd ever seen five-star-cuisine, much less tasted it, but she was sure the tables groaned under its weight. Typical of aliens, a showy over-abundance to demonstrate Rafe's wealth.

Garmood led her to the dance floor with Rafe close on her other side. The guests, two hundred of Rafe's closest friends, stood. Pepper searched the crowd, recognizing human officials and a few friends from work consigned to tables nearest the kitchen and furthest from the blood bar.

There would be no champagne. The aliens thought consuming alcohol a health risk for humans and banned it, along with garlic, silver, and anything else that might be considered dangerous or could poison the blood supply. Pitchers of water congregated beside the cake. Pepper thought the four-tiered, black construction was confectionary. It did have beautiful white roses decorating the base and top.

Garmood roared, rattling everything in the room.

Pepper jumped, her heart so firmly stuck in her throat it stopped her scream. "Kivronians and guests," he boomed. "It is my pleasure to introduce Rafe Nucretah and his mate, Pepper."

The vampires hissed in approval while the humans quaked in a clump near the kitchen door. Pepper couldn't stop trembling. Her crisp silk dress rustled like a bag of potato chips being shaken.

Rafe slipped his arm around her waist and she stilled. Though Pepper barely knew him, she felt comforted by his touch. She hadn't noticed the comfort last night or anytime before the binding. She'd heard the ritual changed you. Was it that, or was she picking up emotions from Rafe, sucking in his calm energy like a black hole?

"Are you up to this?" Rafe held her close, protected under his broad shoulder.

Was she up to anything? Rafe moved her further away from Garmood. "I think so. Yes."

"Then, I'd like you to meet my brother."

She spied him instantly. A dark, handsome man approached dressed in jet-black and almost as tall as Rafe. He had the same sleek, dark hair and the signature good looks, but his eyes held a brooding quality.

Rafe smiled. Not the practiced grin of a politician, but a genuine curve of his lips that lighted his eyes with pleasure.

"Pepper, I'd like to introduce you to my younger brother, Dante."

"My blood." Dante extended his claws and held his right hand to his throat. "For yours."

She'd never seen such a greeting, if that's what it was, and wasn't sure how to respond. "Um, thank you."

Rafe chuckled. "He's offering his life for your protection. The correct response is, 'Life eternal'."

"Do I put my hand to my neck as I say it?

"Yes," said Rafe.

She felt odd, but held her throat and repeated the words with all the seriousness she could muster. Dante nodded, but no smile crossed his mouth. She dropped her hand to her side. "I didn't know Rafe had a brother."

"He has two. Me and Bram."

"Two brothers? How wonderful. I'm an only child." She turned to Rafe and cocked her head. "What else have you kept from me?" she teased. "Is Bram as serious as Dante?"

"No." Rafe's mouth twitched.

"What's he like?"

"He's undisciplined," said Dante.

Rafe laughed. She enjoyed the sound as it played over her

ear, a fountain of water trickling over her arid heart. "What's so funny? Is he a black sheep?"

"Black sheep?" Dante raised a questioning brow.

"I mean, is he wayward, non conventional, a free spirit?"

"Bram is all of that," said Rafe, with a glint of humor in his eye.

Pepper was enjoying the conversation and continued to relax. "When will I meet him?"

"Not tonight," said Rafe. "He's occupied elsewhere, but he promises to make an appearance as soon as he's able"

"I'll be happy to know him. I never had brothers, or sisters either. Is there other family?" As soon as the words left her mouth, her gut told her she should have held her tongue.

Rafe's smile faded. "Only our sire, Cadder." The brothers shared a meaningful glance. "He's currently indisposed."

Pepper's reporter instincts smelled a story behind the cryptic answer and sorrow as well. She wouldn't push. "I hope everything is all right."

"It will be," said Rafe.

Dante bowed. "If you will excuse me, Lord Rafe, I wish you and your mate every happiness, but I have duties to attend to."

"Of course. Excused," said Rafe. "And thank you."

Pepper knew Kivronians had firmly drawn lines of protocol, and the formal exchange excusing Dante was nothing unusual. She watched him leave. Dante was cold compared to Rafe, and his stoic face, difficult to read. But she felt closeness between the brothers. It warmed her to know Kivronian relationships were built on more than duty to race and clan. Genuine affection weighed in, too.

The thoughts of family turned her mind to her father. She'd hoped to find him among the guests as a surprise, but so far, no. "Rafe, have you had any success in bringing my father home?"

He looked uncomfortable and loosened his tie. "Some. I've located him, but he's working for the Supreme High Council, and they mean him to finish before they release him."

"But you've talked to him and he's all right?"

"He's well." He stared past her, distracted. "I've told you all I can."

"Pardon, Lord Rafe." Celeste's perfect exterior appeared frayed as she inserted herself between them. "The President of Mexico is arguing with the Governor of Texas, and they insist you settle the matter."

"Not again." Rafe shook his head.

"Hurry," Celeste urged. "You recall what happened the last time. They never could get all the blood out."

"Forgive me. Duty calls." Rafe kissed Pepper's cheek. "Get something to eat and enjoy yourself. I'll return soon."

Celeste scurried beside Rafe, gesturing wildly. Pepper couldn't hear their conversation, but she caught the gist when Celeste made a slashing motion with her claws.

Vampires. Pepper glanced around the room filled with Kivronians. She'd never fit in with dignitaries, warriors, and bloodthirsty vampires. What place could a human find among them? What place did she have with Rafe? Why had he claimed her? Was the reason that she was a black hole, an unreadable human, a blank space? Standing in the midst of alien supremacy and keenly aware of her shortcomings, she felt like nothing. *A void.* That's what Garmood had called her.

No one looked at her, except the humans nervously chatting a few tables away. A short, portly man stared at his watch and mopped his sweaty brow, those with him were equally rattled. She couldn't blame them. When powerful aliens who drink blood surround you, it's bound to put you on edge. She felt their anxiety, a palpable, erratic vibration that shook her, but she wasn't frightened of being consumed, not like the man checking his watch. Pepper feared being swallowed whole by alien culture, losing all that she was inside, and that she no longer mattered to anyone anywhere.

She had friends, but now bound to Rafe those relationships would change. A few co-workers from the paper braved the celebration. But her best friend, Leanne, was the one bright spot in a sea of indifference. They'd known each other since sixth grade and had shared everything since. Pepper caught her eye and waved.

Leanne grinned back, latched on to a young man's arm and chugged toward her. "Pepper, great party." Leanne's too tight smile broadened. "You look—festive."

"Thanks. It's Kivronian tradition." Pepper tugged on the black silk skirt. "Sorry for the short notice."

"No worries. Congratulations. I hope you'll be very happy." Leanne's grip on the man's arm showed white knuckles. His eyes darted when anyone came within ten feet of them.

Pepper didn't blame them. It was a feat of bravery for Leanne to overcome her timidity of social gatherings to attend. Pepper slipped on her plastic smile. "I'm sure we will be. Who wouldn't be ecstatic over marrying Rafe?"

Leanne fingered the gold crucifix at her neck. "Yes." Her blue gaze fell. "Um. Sorry we can't stay. Early morning, but we'll do lunch."

Pepper had her doubts. Leanne only wore the necklace when her dread of vampires threatened to immobilize her. A crucifix had no effect on the aliens, but silver burned their skin like acid. Anyone in possession of the metal was assigned to work in the blood processing plant. "Promise?"

"Sure." Leanne bobbed like a bobble-head doll. A roar from the blood bar, and Leanne yowled. "We gotta go." A short hug, brief smile, and Leanne bolted for the door, her male escort overtaking her.

Scared, they couldn't escape fast enough. Not a surprise. Leanne had a right to her vampire issues. Only Pepper's father held the trusted position of shield and confidant and he'd been transferred to Kivron. Since the plague and alien occupation, everything had been a struggle. Was her future more of the same? Surviving her marriage, the loss of self, and her life while Rafe conquered her as he had everything else around him. Bound. *Chained.*

Her tongue stuck to the roof of her dry mouth and she moved to the cake table for a drink. Lifting a glass of water, the cold stung her injured thumb still wrapped in black cloth. She'd brought the binding on herself. The chill of the glass ran up her arm. What did binding mean? *Forever,* that she understood. But what else? Was she property, a pet, a wife, or a slave? The chill covered her body.

In a few hours, he'd take her to his home. That much she'd wheedled out of Rafe. Celeste refused to tell her anything, saying it wasn't her place and Lord Nucretah would inform her. But he hadn't.

All she had was conjecture and assumption. It's not wise to base things on flimsy proof, but she had little else to go on. Desperate to string understanding from the threads she knew, Pepper concocted a scenario. He'd expect sex. She'd refuse and they'd argue. Vampires didn't take no for an answer. Her hand trembled and she sipped from her glass. She hoped he'd be gentle and that she could get past being violated. Her skin prickled.

"There you are." Garmood smiled. "How can such a striking woman find herself alone? Where is Nucretah?"

His presence so close on the heels of her upsetting thoughts unnerved her further. She took a moment to breathe. "Rafe should be back in a minute."

Heat from his muscular frame radiated, but it didn't warm her. "I'm concerned for you, my dear. A human tied to Nucretah." Garmood gazed at her with soft, amber eyes. So different from the stalking tiger she'd envisioned earlier. "Has he told you anything about us or your new life?"

"Not much." She'd almost admitted Rafe had told her nothing, but hadn't thought it wise to share personal information with a stranger.

"I didn't think so." Garmood crinkled his broad forehead. "It's not right."

"What?" she could think of a myriad of things that fit that description, the claiming and binding to name just two. Both had been sick and wrong as weddings went.

"The way Nucretah's claimed you. I understand he snatched you up." He looked away. His profile suggested deep thought and then he turned his focus on her. "I feel it my duty to caution you about him."

It was too late for caution. They were bound and that was eternal. "What do I need to know?"

"Many things." Garmood shook his head of thick, red hair, the strands falling over his broad shoulders. "Nucretah should have told you before the binding."

She wanted to ask what, but her intuition told her to let it go. She changed the subject. "What brings you to Red Rock? Nothing here could be worth your attention."

"The official reason? The Supreme High Council commissioned me to negotiate peace with the rebels. Unfortunately, that won't take long."

"Why is that unfortunate? I'd think you'd want to return to Kivron."

"I do, but abuse of power disgusts me. It's my duty to see that the conspirators find mercy. It will go far in maintaining any peace between our people. All humans deserve respect and a chance at freedom."

His words surprised her. Every inch of Garmood exuded fierce warrior. "You're a man of peace?"

"Difficult to believe?" He laughed softly. "Centuries of battle and loss change a man. I've lost my taste for killing."

Something didn't feel right. But was it Garmood, her disquiet over her new life or the continual anxiety vibrating from the humans? She'd never experienced her intuition like this, an open door allowing anything to enter, pieces flying at her from every side. Her head swam with confusion and she rubbed her temple with the fingers of her free hand.

"Are you all right?" Garmood stared at her, the sharp lines of his face lessened by tenderness. The warrior was handsome, not in the same obvious sense as Rafe, but undeniably good looking.

"I'm fine," she lied, and took a sip from her glass. "You said there was an official reason, I take it you have an unofficial reason as well."

"Your sire asked me to come. He wanted to know if Nucretah was your choice."

Her heart pounded and words flew from her mouth. "You've seen my father? Is he all right? When is he coming back?"

"I spoke to him recently. The Council has him on a vital project. He'll return when he's finished."

"When?" She could barely contain her excitement. "Are you now friends?" She trembled and Garmood took her glass before she spilled it.

"Friends? Of a fashion." He pulled out a chair, sat her on it, and crouched beside her. Pepper studied his face, delved into his amber eyes, and looked away. What she'd seen confused her, compassion, desire, and a wound so deep it made her heart ache. "I have an office downstairs where we may talk.

When you're ready, come see me," he said.

She forced her gaze back to his, emotions clogging her throat. "I will."

# # #

Bloodshed averted, Rafe casted about and spied Pepper seated alone. Her lovely face framed by her hair, eyes staring blankly at the windows and the night sky. He doubted she saw the city lights or stars. Striding toward her, he watched her chew at her bottom lip as if concentrating. What was in her head? "Pepper, you're pale. Have you eaten anything?"

She turned from the window and focused on him, green eyes searching. Humans avoided eye contact with Kivronians as a rule, but not her. "No. I've been thinking."

"And?" he prodded.

"What happens now?" The stink of fear oozed from her. "We're bound, but I don't know what I am to you, what's expected of me and this—relationship."

She didn't understand. He ran his hand through his hair. He'd told her to wear the dress, pack and be ready. Had he explained anything else? "We go to our home and begin our thirty nights." Is that what she wanted? He despised not knowing her thoughts.

Her eyes widened. Fear increased and poured from her. "Thirty nights?"

"You've never heard of this?"

She shook her head.

Silch, the madness again. He hadn't explained the betrothal and hadn't remembered to tell Celeste to inform her. What must the girl think? He could only guess from the frightened look in her eyes. He'd have to calm her before she trembled off her chair. "We're bound and now we begin our courtship. In human terms, we're betrothed. You're my espoused wife. We live together, learn about each other and affection is encouraged." Her dress rustled. *She's scared.* "Ease your mind, darling, it's forbidden to consummate the binding before the allotted thirty nights is past."

The rustling quieted. "We're married, but not?"

"We're bound in everyway, but not physically. Did you believe I was a barbarian and would take you before you were willing?" With gaining her trust as his first objective, he had a poor start. He must do better.

"What else could I think?"

"Nothing else. It's my mistake. I should've told you before the binding."

"I might have gotten some sleep last night if you had." Her lips curved into a small smile.

He commandeered a chair, sat beside her and took her hand, threading her fingers with his. "I've no excuse for my thoughtless behavior. Will you forgive me?"

She stared at him, chewing on that full bottom lip he wanted to kiss. "No sex?"

"Affection only."

"Oh." She relaxed against the back of her chair. "What else should you tell me?" She tilted her head, the fall of her hair revealing the soft skin of her neck on one side.

How he wanted to press his mouth to that skin, breathe in her scent of soap perfumed with herbs. At least, that was allowed. What should he tell her? A hundred things burdened him, the truth of his condition, the madness plaguing him, and how desperately he needed her love to cure him. He couldn't tell her any of that. "What do you want to know?"

She pursed her lips. "What happens after the thirty nights?"

"We consummate and begin our life together for then we are fully bound. "

"What if I'm not—ready?" She stared at their joined hands.

Not ready? He'd never entertained the idea. Of course she'd be ready to love him. He'd woo her, compliment her and whisper words of love to her under the stars. Why wouldn't she be ready? He couldn't demand her affection. Scaring her would be counterproductive. He couldn't fight this war with aggression and win. He swore to himself. He'd have to win in another way.

Rafe raised her hand to his lips and kissed her knuckles. "Darling, then I'll wait." He couldn't wait. He'd be dead.

CHAPTER FIVE

Fear was a strange thing. It ebbed and flowed like the tide. Rising up with fierce waves, submerging Pepper's common sense and drowning wisdom. When it receded, she looked at what it left, a grimy, damp residue affecting who she was, and how she thought. Memories from deep within her were dragged up and left on the shore of her mind to be picked up, studied, and valued or discarded.

Rafe's claim had stirred up an ocean's worth of unresolved pain and fear, and deposited it in her nervous hands. No way to throw it back. The binding was eternal. She'd have to deal with the relationship forced on her and the dull ache in her heart for those she'd lost.

The decision to barter herself for her father wasn't brave. She shook her head. It wasn't a sacrifice either. Purely selfish, she'd accepted Rafe and made the deal to quiet the panic clutching her chest. Too much loss made her tremble at the thought of caring for anyone. Easier to wall up her heart against tender feelings that made it difficult to survive, much less to flourish in a world where aliens ruled. She's had little choice of where she'd lived, what she'd eaten, and now, whom she'd marry.

No one to blame for her situation, except herself. She was responsible for her actions. And her feelings. She did her best to stifle emotions that made life difficult. Love eventually ended in death, and she refused to experience that grief ever again. The only way to avoid it was never to care, never to love, never to be open to the devotion that had ripped out her heart in the past. Fear could be used as a protection.

She wasn't proud of considering fear a tool. Acting from that insecure place was cowardly. It's why humanity had given up without a fight when the aliens had invaded. They'd all lost so much, they would rather surrender than suffer more. Because humanity had feared, they had given up their freedom. Her stomach knotted. *I've done the same.*

In the entry of Rafe's mansion Pepper stood alone with her thoughts, waiting as he conferred with Dante in another room. A reclusive movie star had owned the home until the aliens had come, evicted the aging actress, and had confiscated the property. Pepper shifted on her black pumps. Remnants of the original style remained, brown marble floors and cathedral ceilings, windows designed to take advantage of mountain views and light.

Changed by vampire needs, heavy russet drapes covered the windows to guard against sun, and sealed off natural beauty. Dim illumination, sufficient for alien eyes, cast everything in muted grays. Dark paintings of Kivron hung on the vanilla walls and a grotesque sculpture that appeared to be dipped in blood oppressed the center of the immense space. *And this is home.* A shiver skittered down her back.

She adjusted the bag containing her treasures in her arms. Holding it comforted her. And she needed comfort. When Rafe brought her father home, she hoped the binding would be worth it. She clasped the sack close to her chest. Rafe had wanted to carry it for her and asked to have it sent ahead, but she'd refused, needing it close so her fingers could touch her memories, the love and peace that evaded her now.

"Pepper." Rafe strode in tailed by Dante, and smiled, his eyes sparkling. "Allow me to show you the house and then take you to your room."

Your room. Tension slipped from her neck. Not *our* room, but hers. A private space. "Is Dante joining us?"

"No, but when you're in your room, he'll be posted outside."

"Do you think I'll make a break for it?" It had crossed her mind.

He licked his delicious lips. "My brother is afraid I'll sneak in and make passionate love to you."

She wobbled on her pumps, fearing Rafe would do just that, and hoping he might. *The binding*. It had to be affecting her. Any woman would find him attractive. The man was the stuff of legend, but she couldn't afford for her emotions to become entangled with him. The binding, *no*, business agreement, had to remain clear in her head. She couldn't mean anything to him. Falling for his handsome face, charm, and sophistication could only end in agony for her.

# # #

Rafe escorted Pepper through the house. How should woo the girl? Had he known Pepper, bedded her before the claim and binding, she'd already adore him. There'd be no pressure. It wasn't arrogance, but confidence in his skill as a lover that irritated him in the situation. Had madness not clouded his mind, had Hebric's end not demanded action, Rafe would've thought it through and done differently.

When he brushed against her soft curves and smelled her fresh and alluring scent, which fed his increasing need, he wondered how he would endure the betrothal. *Affection only.* He couldn't recall halting at affection when he'd wanted a woman. Did he know how? At some point, arousal took over. His goal had always been sex. Not once had his agenda been love. Humans were erratic enough without bringing emotion into it. Seducing women came second nature to him. He'd have to slow down, watch himself before going too far. With insanity blunted, but not expelled, he must guard Pepper's life and his chance to be whole.

Rafe showed her the kitchen, the living room, the dining area, the media center, and on. The space was ridiculously large for his needs. His position required a show of strength and opulence. *The conquered must never forget their place,* another Kivronian dictate. That law wouldn't help him win Pepper.

She avoided his gaze, didn't speak, and cemented her arms to the bag she clutched, as if it contained something priceless. Humans owned little of value. What trinkets she harbored meant something to her. She hid herself behind them like a shield.

He smiled at her. She looked away. He brushed against her. She flinched. *Flinched.* Was he disgusting, an unsavory creature best left in a pit? If only he could read the woman's mind. He breathed in, searching for information, and detected not the sharp scent of panic, but of anxiety and worry. The scents were similar, but he knew the tang of one from the other.

He led her outside to the patio and gardens. The property had been styled after an Italian villa. Pepper's human eyes wouldn't see much of it in the dark, but the night air might help him to focus. As he directed her attention to a series of fountains, he stole a glance at her. Pepper's long hair moved in the breeze, caressing her face and bare shoulders. He ached to touch her soft skin under the stars, to kiss her into submission, and to take all he desired, but he'd wait. Pouncing on her like prey would destroy them both. *Patience.* "You did well," he said, wanting to compliment her on something other than her appearance.

"The binding?" She shrugged. "I survived it."

"You have courage." His fingers itched to slide over her satin skin.

Her eyes shot up to his face and then turned away. "No, not courage," she murmured, hugging her belongings to her chest. "I did what I had to."

At least she was talking, and he took that as a small victory. "Was it what you expected?"

She chewed at her bottom lip again and stared at the stone floor. "Blood didn't surprise me, but having to taste yours did." She shuddered.

He stopped himself, before complimenting her delicious flavor. Better steer her mind away from what he fed on. "I won't see you until tomorrow evening. I have work early, but then I'm free to spend time with you."

"You don't have to."

"I want to."

"Why?" She focused on a stray weed pushing up through a crack in the pavement and nudged it with her toe. "We're not having sex, so why would you rearrange your life?"

"I want to know you."

"Why? What's in it for you?"

He wasn't used to explaining himself, and certainly not to humans. With his patience thinning, and frustration mounting, heightened by insanities' prodding, his fangs appeared. "I'm through with questions," he growled. "We're bound. Reason enough."

"Fine," she shouted, and scowled at him, chin raised in defiance.

He'd killed men for less. But looking at Pepper, and at the

fear in her eyes as she challenged him, Rafe tamped down his irritation, and tightened his mouth against the string of oaths he wanted to roar. *Patience.* He struggled against insanity and gained control. "I'll show you to your room."

Anger had overcome her fear long enough for her to shout at him. No one dared speak to him that way. Not since he'd been a whelp, and then he'd deserved it. *Stubborn, annoying woman.*

They walked in silence with Pepper lagging behind. His response to her inane questions hadn't been well received. What did she expect, answers? He couldn't admit the madness had forced his claim and compelled him to win her love. *Show no weakness.* They stood at her bedroom door. "This is your room. Everything you need has been supplied."

"Humph," she grunted, refusing to look at him.

It took what remained of his composure, but he ignored her rude noise, and left her in the hall.

# # #

Pepper stomped into the bedroom, caught the door before it slammed and closed it gently. She wouldn't sink to his level and act like a child. For a species that prided itself on control, Rafe had precious little. Apparently, control was what they wielded over others, not over themselves. She'd wondered who the real Rafe was, and now she had a good idea. "Obstinate, arrogant, insufferable alien. Growling at her like a…a…vampire."

She trudged to the bed and placed her bag on the sage green comforter. The room was extravagant. Huge, tall ceilings with a brown and green marble fireplace imposed on one wall. "Always the best for the aliens," she muttered, as she sat on the bed and kicked off her pumps.

He'd bound her. What else did he want? A relationship? "Huh." Not him. The man wouldn't answer a simple question. Why did he want to know her? If that mattered, he'd have taken the time to do it before making his claim. No, he *needed* to bind someone to him. She'd just happened to walk in at the wrong moment. *Lucky me.*

The man was hedging. She felt him trying to avoid a direct reply to her question, because he had no answer. He'd lied that he wanted to spend time with her just like the other deceptions the vampires spouted. *Keep humans happy, docile. Promise them anything and then renege.* Why should she expect anything different from him?

She got to her feet and peeled off her dress, leaving it on

the floor. Staring at the black clump of fabric brought tears to her eyes. This was her wedding night? What a disaster. The dress was wrong, the ceremony wrong, the groom wrong and wrong again. She clenched her fists, standing on the chocolate carpet in her black lace underwear. *I'm wrong.*

They hadn't been bound twenty-four hours and already they'd argued. How would she put up with that man? *For my father.* She'd put up with almost anything to bring her father home and to know he was safe. Too many people had transferred to Kivron and had never been heard from again. She knew something was off. If Rafe kept his word in this one thing, she'd tolerate the binding. Being able to talk with her father over breakfast, laughing as he teased her about burned toast, it would all be worth it.

She padded to the bathroom, chocolate marble, floor to ceiling, elegant fixtures, and a shower large enough to waltz in. *I didn't even get to dance.* As a young girl, she'd dreamed of dancing in her husband's arms at their reception. She dropped her underwear to the floor. Her hopes of a wedding, a reception and love had ended when Josh had died.

Eighteen was a fragile age, so much optimism, open to everything and vulnerable. Even after losing her mother, she'd believed that somehow the plague wouldn't take Josh from her. He'd been strong, only twenty-two. Their love would tip the scales and he'd make it.

A silly, immature dream, love doesn't cure anything. It couldn't save her mother, her friends, and it hadn't saved Josh. Pepper turned on the shower and stepped under the warm stream, closing her eyes to block the anguish of the past, and wished the spray could wash everything away.

As Pepper dried her hair, she turned her mind to the large amber-eyed dignitary. Garmood's fierce appearance unnerved her. The memory of his growling at her father frightened her, but when Garmood bothered to speak to her at the reception, it said something for him. Had he changed from the man she'd spied years ago? It took humility for high-ranking Kivronians to treat humans as equals, and he'd sought her out. Pepper, well aware of her standing with the aliens, had felt Garmood's sincerity when he'd warned her about Rafe.

Wrapping a towel around her damp body, she shuffled to the bedroom and huddled in a chair before the fireplace, beautiful, but cold without a crackling blaze. What sort of man was Rafe that a Kivronian would take time to warn a human about him? *Short tempered.* That she'd seen. *Impatient.* His quick claim proved that. Was Rafe also violent and capable of doing her physical harm? Her intuition didn't confirm that fear, but she'd misread signs before.

She recalled the look on Garmood's face, and how the harsh lines had softened as he spoke to her. He'd been kind. Did he only look like a dangerous tiger? Rafe appeared charming and well-mannered, but tonight she'd witnessed irritation and threat. Each had cautioned her about the other. *Who'd lied?*

Pepper pulled her knees to her chest and adjusted the towel to cover her legs. *Maybe both played a game and used her against the other.* That she'd believe. Gaining information would help her sort things out. Rafe refused to answer her questions, but Garmood had invited her to visit, talk, and explain things no one else seemed willing to discuss. She ran her fingers through her hair untangling the thick strands. Tomorrow, she'd visit Garmood.

# # #

Rafe strode down the hall and down the stairs. Dante waited at the bottom and watched, but nothing showed in his expression. "Lord Rafe, you seem perturbed. Isn't it going well?"

He wanted to roar, but spoke in quiet even tones. "She's impossible."

"She's human."

"She's impossible for a human."

Dante's measured stare annoyed Rafe. He saw too much through those dark eyes. "What did she do?"

"Questioned me. Can you imagine? She doubted when I told her I wanted to know her."

"Do you?"

"I must," he grumbled. "You're aware that I've only until the end of the betrothal to win her heart."

Dante folded his arms over his battle-suit clad chest. "I've seen you win women's hearts in three hours, thirty nights is more than ample time for a man like you. Why did she doubt you?"

Rafe strode to the living room and paced the expanse of Persian carpet, Dante followed. "How should I know? The girl's a black hole."

"They exist?"

"Apparently, and I've bound myself to one." Rafe took another lap around the room. "I can't pick up anything from her head."

"If you can't read her thoughts, how are you going to know her preferences and win her affection?"

Rafe stared at Dante, his frustration simmering. "Excellent question. I'll have to court the woman, but she declines my company. I don't have time for her female games."

"This is difficult."

"Yes."

"I'm curious, when she questioned you, how did you respond?"

Rafe's temper flared, but he maintained control and only growled. "I told her that we're bound and that's reason enough to spend time together."

"I see." Dante rubbed his chin.

"What's that supposed to mean?"

"I think I see the problem."

Rafe halted pacing and glared at his younger brother. "I didn't realize you were an authority on human females."

Dante almost smiled, a rare occurrence. "I have an opinion."

Rafe lowered himself onto the overstuffed, buff couch. "Well, then enlighten me."

"She's human and seeks to understand her situation. It isn't as if we've been open with humanity."

Rafe ran his hand hard through his hair. "I've explained the binding and betrothal. That's more than most humans know. What else could she want?"

"If I were to guess, and I'm no expert on women, I'd say she needs reassurance from you."

"What, that I care for her? That's the entire purpose for spending time together, so I might prove it and gain her love."

"What have you done so far?"

Tension crept up Rafe's neck and into his head, a steady throbbing at the base of his brain. "I claimed her, bound her, and chose the woman above any other. That's not enough for her to know I want her?"

"It was abrupt."

"There was no choice. And what's that got to do with it?"

"Human females require reassurance. Since you bound her, what have you done to woo the girl?"

Rafe shook his head wearily. "I'm forbidden to make love to her and she's not out for fame or fortune. Pepper only wants her father returned from Kivron. If at all possible, I'll accomplish ithat. Since we were bound, I've complimented her courage, but she denied it, and then we argued. How do you propose I convince and court her, bring her those weeds humans are fond of?"

"It's worth considering, and I believe they're called flowers."

Was the universe determined to try his patience? "I know what they're called. We have acres of them growing on the property."

"Take her some." Dante cleared his throat and looked away. "And apologize."

"What?" Rafe jumped to his feet. "No. Absolutely not. I won't admit weakness."

"You should."

"I'm to ask forgiveness?"

"Yes. Human women seem to like it."

Rafe's head was ready to explode. "I won't do it."

Dante stared at him. "Are you still suffering effects of madness, the muddled thoughts, headaches, and the voices?"

Rafe's mouth went dry. "You know?"

"Of course, you're my brother." Dante put his hand on Rafe's shoulder, demonstrative for him. "Then, apologize. Tell her she was right and you were wrong."

"You expect me to humble myself."

"I expect my courageous brother to do what he must to win her and survive."

Rafe rubbed his eyes, feeling the weight of exhaustion drag on his body. "It's a hard thing."

"You've overcome more distressing situations."

Rafe focused on his brother. "But I wasn't half insane at the time."

CHAPTER SIX

Everything appeared brighter in the light of day. That's what her mother had always said. Pepper drank her black coffee, breathing in pine-scented air between sips from her father's old, blue mug. The patio overlooked the gardens. It calmed her ragged nerves to listen to leaves rustle in the breeze, while she relaxed with the autumn sun pouring over her face.

Rafe and Dante were nowhere to be seen. She smiled, glad for the solitude and the respite from the unusual onslaught of intuition. Pepper planned to go into town to see Garmood, and after Rafe's tirade last night, she was even more determined. She should learn more about the red-haired warrior before trusting him. After mining all available leads, she'd sort them out later. Unbiased sources were what she needed, but when it came to the aliens, she doubted any such sources existed. Everything skewed to make them look good.

As she enjoyed the peace of the outdoors, Pepper contemplated her situation. It hadn't been her plan to marry a vampire. She hadn't counted on ever marrying anyone, not after Josh died. Heat from the mug warmed her fingers, but didn't touch the ball of ice rolling in her gut. Loving Josh had only made losing him unbearable.

She took a sip from the steaming cup and tryed to melt her frigid insides. Arguing with Rafe had been a stupid mistake. She knew it when she opened her eyes this morning. How could she expect favors from the man if she irritated him? Why couldn't she be like most women and cheerfully agree with the aliens, even when they were wrong?

It wasn't in her nature to tolerate being abused in any way. She clenched her jaw. Rafe had been rude. *I hate rudeness.* It made her crazy and she usually retorted with a quip she regretted afterward. She'd held her tongue with him. No sarcastic jibe had passed her lips. At least, she hadn't intended to annoy him.

Rafe had started out reasonable. His outburst was her fault. She'd pushed him with her reporter, need-to-know questions. Could she curb her inquisitive nature? She'd have to if she wanted her father home. She could be pleasant and charming. Pepper rehearsed her plastic smile. *Would he buy it? Why not?* She was a black hole. Rafe wouldn't be able to tell whether she had a change of heart or not.

After her father returned, she'd find the courage to make the best of her new life. A real smile replaced the fake. He'd always been her safe place, the voice of reason that got her through when things fell apart. The smile faded. With her father gone, she felt unprepared to deal with Rafe, but she had to try.

As vampires went, Rafe was decent. Her relentless need to guard her heart had her fixed on finding his negative traits so she could push him away and justify her distance. She shook her head. *Find* negative traits? No, she'd invent them if she had to. She'd done it before to any man who'd gotten too close. It wasn't fair to them. Her father had told her that it wasn't fair to her, either. The ice in her stomach chilled her and she pulled her gray jacket close around with her free hand.

It wouldn't kill her to focus on Rafe's strengths and it might improve her attitude. She could smile at him and act gracious. She would subjugate her fear of being hurt to get her father home.

Pepper started by mentally listing the obvious. Rafe was undeniably handsome, charismatic, and sexy. He had a rich, velvet voice that curled her toes. She liked that. Great protective instincts, he'd removed her from Garmood when she'd trembled from his roar. Generous. She ran her hand over her thigh covered in fine gray slacks. Rafe had loaded her closet with new clothes in her size. Until now, her wardrobe had consisted of second hand items. He didn't have to do that. *What else?* She crinkled her forehead in thought. *Was he kind?* She didn't think vampires valued kindness, but he had a close relationship with his brother. *Promising.*

She leaned back in the black wrought iron chair, the metal pressing against her spine, and sipped from her mug. "Ugh." *Luke warm.* She set the cup on the ground by her feet. Rafe was polished perfection on the outside. But underneath, what would she find? There were moments when she felt she knew things about him. It might be her imagination, but it didn't feel like it. Thoughts and feelings sunk into her brain that didn't belong to her, but they flew away before she could consider them. She'd always trusted her gut, but her awareness about Rafe was peculiar. A connection deeper than a feeling, it was knowledge coming in words, and pictures. And it seemed to be increasing. Did the binding do that? If she could hold on to her intuition to know why he'd claimed her, and why he'd rushed everything, it would help. Understanding always helped. Information was key.

Did she want to dig beneath his attractive surface to learn the truth? Understanding Rafe required time together and each moment together could bring her closer to caring for him. Her gut twisted. Caring skated dangerously close to love and she shied away from that precipice, but something compelled her to feel more for him than was comfortable. It had to be the binding, maybe ingesting vampire blood, perhaps both. She had to guard herself, if she could.

When Rafe said he wanted to know her, did he desire a relationship or just want to satisfy his curiosity? Did it matter? If spending time with Rafe sped her father's return, then she'd devote every waking moment to him. The risk to her heart made her tremble and she shoved down her fear. How difficult could it be? Rafe ruled the Western Quadrant and had constant demands on his time. She could smile through a few dinners. And while the betrothal ticked by, she'd hunt up information, interview Garmood, and focus her intuition to learn what Rafe hid from her. She shook her head. *Was that possible*? Could she learn to hone in and dissect one thought from another and make sense of it? She had nothing better to do. No job to occupy her, no family, only her thoughts, her intuition, and the alien who'd bound her.

An hour later, Pepper waited outside Garmood's office on the main floor of the government complex, the same building Rafe ruled from. Every few minutes her skin prickled and she glanced over her shoulder, feeling someone staring. She half-expected to find Rafe behind her, indignant, and glaring with his fangs protruding. He'd disapprove of her meeting Garmood. Those two obviously didn't like each other, but since Rafe refused to talk, she had little other choice to learn about her husband.

Would the red-haired warrior be honest? She trusted her gut to catch a lie. Speaking with Garmood, she'd learn something about him as well, even if he hedged on her questions. Pepper prepared to gather facts. She wasn't sure how to proceed, but her instincts tended to point her in the right direction.

Garmood's caution concerning Rafe had intrigued her, pulling at her thoughts, refusing to let go. Was it the warning that compelled her or the hope that Garmood would supply ammunition to justify walling up her emotions from Rafe? She fisted her hands in her lap and shifted on the chair. She knew the answer. *I'm such a coward.*

A tall, dark-haired man in a battle-suit winked at her as he strode past on his way to the desk. He stared at her too long, his eyes traveling over her with interest. She wanted to look away, but didn't. She glared at him. He smiled and then was ushered into Garmood's office. *Presumptive, arrogant alien.* The man's swagger and long, dark waves screamed *bad boy*. In a world plentiful with alien, male perfection, there were variations on that theme. Rafe was a nice guy compared to that specimen.

She'd waited for hours when Garmood's secretary, a slender blond man, called her to his desk. "Lord Garmood Loth can't see you today, but he's available in...let me see...." The alien's thin fingers slid over the screen. "Yes, three days from now."

She blinked. "That's the earliest?"

"Yes. You didn't have an appointment. Should I schedule you?"

"Please."

He didn't bother to look at her, typical. The aliens either paid too much attention or next to none. *Irritating.* She should be used to it by now. "Excuse me, but did that man have an appointment?"

He stared at her down his snub nose, annoyed. "All

warriors report to Lord Garmood upon arrival to the quadrant."

"Thank you." She flashed her plastic smile, realizing she'd be depending on that fake persona frequently to get her father home. She'd better get used to it.

# # #

Rafe had left his office early loaded with gifts to surprise Pepper. Tropical flowers and chocolates were difficult to come by and he'd spent half the morning tracking them down. Celeste hadn't approved of his zeal or his foisting upon her the search for pointless human delicacies. He'd bound the girl, done. Though Rafe agreed with Celeste in sentiment, he had to try every route available to Pepper's heart. He couldn't afford her anger, not with each night bringing him closer to insanity and execution.

He glared at the blooms in the crystal vase, Birds of Paradise, interspersed with some, red waxy flowers, and fragrant Plumeria. The impressive bouquet had yet to be received. Where was she? His driver and the Bentley were gone. Pepper had left him a note saying she'd be home by dinner, but nothing about where she'd gone or with whom. He wanted to shred the weeds taunting him from the dining table.

Was he a fool as Celeste had suggested? Her derisive words, spurred by his insane whispers, fueled impatience. *Silch*. He dared not entertain anything that edged him closer to pushing her away. He'd done a fine job of that already.

He couldn't tolerate her disregard for the binding and rules of betrothal. She was his mate, untried, but still she couldn't run loose unprotected, not before completion of the thirty nights. She was putting all their lives in jeopardy. Any savvy, Kivronian male might take the opportunity to challenge Rafe's claim and seize her. Insanity would then combine with his fury and none would be safe, least of all Pepper.

He strode past the dining table laden with gifts and outside to the garden. The sun had set but only a few stars shone in the darkening sky. He needed space, peace, something to set his mind and body right. The fatigue and voices had lessoned at the binding, but he felt them inching forward with slow, determined effort. Thirty nights to gain Pepper's love, and she could barely stand his company. It had to change, and soon.

Every moment she stayed away revved up the madness and his determination against his enemy. In his thirst for revenge, Garmood was a likely culprit to take Pepper from him, disregarding the destruction that would follow. If insanity hadn't gripped Rafe, the stakes would still be high enough, but now, if he lost her, he'd need to be exterminated before he annihilated everyone within reach.

Garmood wanted her. Rafe saw it in his scheming, yellow eyes, the lust for her body and blood. Pepper would have to agree to his advances, and accept his right to challenge Rafe's claim. Not in battle with Nova swords or in claw-to-claw combat, Rafe would welcome such an opportunity. Then the loser would die and the winner would take all.

This challenge left him little control. The outcome wasn't within his power to secure. His body thrummed with anger. Both males were allowed to court. In the end, the woman would decide between them. The victor lived out his long life with her, while the defeated survived in agony for centuries, knowing the woman he loved bore his enemy's children. Rafe's chest constricted to the point of pain. It's how his sire had taken his mother from Garmood.

This situation had little resemblance to his parents. Humans couldn't bear Kivronian children, and Pepper would never accept Garmood's advances. The monster terrified her. And the other option, that she would prefer that snake to Rafe was unthinkable. She'd never negate their binding by making her plea and swearing love to Garmood. *Would she?*

Rafe shook himself away from the disturbing thoughts. He'd protect against losing his rights to her. If need be, he'd post guards around Pepper. Garmood couldn't be allowed to accomplish his goal. Rafe would patiently explain the danger of her actions. But how, without admitting to madness? *I'll think of something.*

First he'd make amends for last night or she wouldn't listen to him. After she accepted his apology, they'd stroll the garden and he'd steal a kiss. Before she had time to protest, he'd continue to lull her body into compliance until she ached for him. A worthy assault against that fortress she'd erected.

Why had she built protection? Fear and desire warred in her flashing green eyes. But what had devastated her that she denied her attraction to him? He sensed it, smelled the want, and felt her rapid pulse when he drew near. Yes, there was fear, but also the lust of longing. She wanted him—badly. Had life been so difficult that she'd numbed her emotions, leaving her unaware of her own needs? Had someone hurt her? That would account for her resistance. If that were the case, he'd have to thaw her out. He smiled, confident in his skills to ignite her frigid interior. Once he'd awakened her passion, it would be simple to gain her love. The plan had to work.

# # #

All Pepper wanted was a bite of food, a hot bath, and then
to barricade herself in her room with a good book. The thought
of putting up with Rafe's attitude didn't appeal to her. She'd
had enough frustration for one day. When she entered the
foyer of the mansion, she knew by the soft music that Rafe was
home. There'd be no sneaking up to her room. The man might
not be able to read her mind, but his acute hearing and sense of
smell would give her away.

"Pepper," Rafe called, his velvet voice meeting her before
her eyes adjusted to the dim light.

She blinked to focus. He stood before her, every inch the
powerful, seductive vampire. *Damn. I'm caught.* She forced a
smile. "Hello."

His mouth held a rigid line. "I...was waiting."

She looked away, slid her purse from her shoulder, and
placed it on the table along the wall. "I'm here." Tired and
hungry, she gathered her energy and continued her plastic
grin. "I left a note. Is there a problem?"

"I was concerned."

She stared in disbelief. "Why?" She'd only been gone for

the afternoon.

"Until the betrothal's complete it's unwise to leave without me."

"Unwise?" A carefully chosen word. "Is that a threat?" It felt like one. He stepped closer. She felt the heat of his body. It made her heart flutter, but she held her ground.

"Not from me," he said, in a voice that caressed like gentle fingers stroking her skin.

Everything about Rafe threatened her, from his enticing, spicy scent calling her to breathe him in, to his sultry look that melted her insides. She refused to let him know it and lifted her chin. "What danger could there be in downtown Red Rock with your Kivronian driver?" She saw the muscles in his jaw work. She was doing it again, asking questions of a man used to giving orders, expecting adherence. What was she thinking? She needed to stay on his good side.

A struggle ensued behind his eyes, darkness giving way to light. "I've warned you about Garmood."

"Is that it? I'm under house arrest because there's bad blood between you and that dignitary?"

"You comprehend?" His provoking lips a kiss away.

"Not really." Warmth flooded her belly. She wished he'd

move and let her breathe. "I know you believe Garmood's dangerous, but I can't endure being locked up."

Rafe captured her gaze. "It's for your protection."

She swallowed, unnerved by his mouth's proximity to hers. His air of command broached no argument. Her gut whispered, *trust him*, but her inquisitive nature, and protective walls wouldn't allow her to follow blindly. And it's what he demanded. "What am I supposed to do here, alone?"

"Not alone. You'll be with me."

Her breath stilled in her chest. "Don't you have to work?"

"I'm taking time off. I want to know you." His lips brushed against the corner of her mouth. "I mean what I say."

Her heart pounded and her knees felt weak. His smoldering gaze was lethal. She wanted to look away, extricate herself from the desire warming her blood, but couldn't. He slid his arm around her waist and pulled her against him, his other hand cradling her head. Her body reacted in spite of her mental protests, tilting her chin, parting her lips in an invitation she couldn't control. His warm mouth covered hers. She opened to his tongue's plea for entrance. This was a bad idea. She knew it. While her defenses buckled under his efforts, her mind fogged and she leaned into him, her arms sliding around his neck. She trembled with want, with passion, and with the fear of her own need.

Her fingers moved to his thick dark hair, twisting in the silky strands as she moaned into his mouth. He deepened the kiss, taking her firmly, owning her mouth with the distinct demand for more. Fear shriveled under the heat of his hands. Her fortress couldn't stand against this and she knew it. But before her walls crumbled, Rafe pulled away, his honeyed taste still on her lips.

"Do you forgive me?" he whispered against her mouth.

"For what?" She couldn't think.

He chuckled softly. "Last night."

What happened last night? She dragged herself from the haze. They'd argued. What had mattered then barely registered with his arms around her. "Oh, that." She waited for her head to clear. "We should talk about this." He nuzzled the sensitive spot on her neck and reason faded.

# # #

Rafe halted his advance down Pepper's soft neck. She'd folded against him in ardent surrender, heightening his desire and the difficulty to pull back. Each moan from her drove him to plunder her willing flesh, but lust wasn't love. He knew the truth of that. Satisfying superficial needs wouldn't gain him the depth of her soul. It would end in insanity. "Are you hungry?"

She blinked up at him with drowsy eyes. "Starved," she mumbled.

A woman shouldn't look so inviting. She shouldn't incite his need so easily, not when he had to curb his instincts and the madness demanding he take her. "I have dinner for us."

The dining table had been laid with china and gold utensils. They gleamed under the candlelight. He seated her and took a chair beside her. Rafe sipped from his crystal goblet, and then wiped his lips with a napkin, careful to remove all crimson residue from his mouth. He wanted her relaxed and unguarded. "How is the lobster?"

"I've never tasted anything like it." She licked her lips, dipped another morsel into the melted butter, and groaned as she chewed. "And the steak, I haven't seen that since before the plague."

Each time she opened her tempting mouth and inserted the fork, he stifled a groan of his own. The thirty-nights would kill him. "I'm glad you're enjoying it."

"I am." She grinned and popped in another bite.

"I want you to feel at home and content around me."

She stopped chewing, stared at him, and then swallowed. "Thank you again for the flowers. They're lovely."

"You're welcome. I've a few tokens for you, but they can wait until after dinner and a walk in the garden."

"Oh." She focused on cutting her steak.

Reading her mind would aid him now. He'd never realized how much he depended on mind reading until he'd met Pepper. Regardless of his lack, he had to combat her nervousness and dismantle her barriers. If talking would help, he'd take part. "I served as General in the Kivronian Civil War."

She looked up from her meal, her brow crinkled. "I'd heard it was brutal. Many of you lost family."

A weight sat on his chest. He hadn't intended to discuss what he'd lost or how, but if it brought him victory, he'd suffer the memories. "First, my mother. She starved sustaining Dante and my sisters. Bram and I were away fighting." The weight increased, crushing his lungs.

"How awful," she murmured, and pushed away her plate.

"Yes."

"And your sisters, did they starve too?" Her eyes glistened with moisture.

He shook his head against the memory. "They died later."

"How many?"

"Including my mother, five."

"I'm sorry." Her chin trembled. "Does the pain ever get better?"

"I miss them." His voice choked in his throat and he cleared it. "It doesn't haunt me continually as it did." Sympathy shimmered in her eyes. He didn't deserve her compassion. The losses had been his fault. But he did need her love. "I haven't forgotten my promise to you."

She sat quiet for a few moments, pushing the food around on her plate. Her eyes lifted. "Any news?"

Based on her expression he guessed her thoughts. "It may be months before the Council releases your father, but I'm working on obtaining leave for him."

Hope replaced the sympathy in her eyes. "Oh, Rafe, if I could see him for a few days."

"I've asked for longer."

"What are the chances?"

Lying to family was against his ethics, but so was tearing apart those he cared for. He'd caused enough pain getting himself captured in the war, and wouldn't willfully hurt her.

"They're good." He sipped from his glass, but the blood had grown cool and thick, as distasteful as the lie.

"I'm finished," she said. "Can we go on that walk? I need some fresh air."

He got to his feet, wanting to leave the subject behind. As they strolled in the garden, the fresh aromas of sage, pine, lavender and scrub oak invigorated him. They walked, hands linked, under the stars. He'd shared more than was comfortable about his past, but not all. Would she ever love him enough to accept the ugly truth? Best to focus on one problem at a time.

"You've never asked me about myself," she said, as they neared the pond.

"I was waiting until you were ready." They stopped to gaze at the mirror surface of the water reflecting the night sky.

"Losing my mother was difficult." Pepper kept her eyes on the pool. "She'd been sick for weeks. My father tried everything to save her." Rafe squeezed her hand in reassurance. "She'd never been strong. I held myself together for him. My father needed me."

"You know loss," Rafe whispered.

She nodded, and focused on the water. "I had a fiancé."

Rafe closed his eyes. That was it, the pain and fear that kept her from him. "The plague?"

"Yes. I thought because we were young and strong, he'd make it."

"There are times when strength isn't enough," he said, gazing at her profile, her face was pale as moonlight and softly captivating.

"Many people died, but…." Her voice broke. "I believed my love could save him." She stared at Rafe. Her mouth held a tremulous smile. "Isn't that silly?"

His heart wrenched. "You lost faith in love?"

"I grew up." She released his hand. "I'm cold. Let's go inside."

CHAPTER SEVEN

Why had she set her pain before him? Was it a sympathetic response to Rafe's loss or to the binding? Pepper rubbed her temples with her fingers to ward off a tension headache. The living room felt familiar and human. Overstuffed, tan furniture, ochre walls, and mahogany tables brought warmth back to her bones. The fireplace of veined burgundy and cream stone, blazed to life when Rafe pushed the button on the side of the mantel.

She soaked in the heat trying to dispel the chill of their conversation. Had she lost her senses? How could she keep him from touching her heart when she opened it to him? He'd shared his loss of family, his strangled voice proving their deaths still affected him, and his haunted, deep brown gaze brought tears to her eyes. Could she guard against his anguish? Naturally she reached out to anyone in need. And his need for love and acceptance drilled holes in her façade. *Damn my tenderness.*

For whatever reason, her intuition had been heightened. His emotions wrapped around her heart and squeezed until she had to fight her desire to comfort him. She struggled between compassion and tears at having invited him in, and admitting her ridiculous belief in love, her childish vulnerability, and her disappointment.

They'd exposed their scars. Had he viewed her as clearly as she'd seen him? It frightened her. She'd absorbed his pain, mopping it up with her emotions like savory gravy. *I still feel it.* Anxiety lay heavy in her chest, invading her sanctuary, and clinging to her.

Along with his agony came guilt, the sharp misery stabbing like a knife in her gut. She'd slept with that discomfort after Josh died. *Why him?* Why hadn't she contracted plague and died? Why had her friends and her mother all succumbed? And the guilty pangs of a twisting blade when she gazed at her father, wracked with grief over her mother's loss.

She lifted her eyes to Rafe, a powerful man. Outwardly in full control, but within there was a gaping wound, bleeding for lack of forgiveness or whatever was left unhealed inside. What caused it? Pepper sucked in a breath, as if the action of pulling air into her lungs would bring her feelings with it, safeguarding them. It didn't work. Dealing with his suffering left her bruised. *I can't do this.* Unshed tears burned behind her eyes.

"Is there something wrong?" Rafe's brow wrinkled.

Everything and nothing. The man had hidden depths. Rafe hurt as she did, and needed. *Like me.* "Just a headache."

"Allow me." He moved closer, touched between her eyes and pressed with his thumb gently. Tightness gave way to relaxation. "Better?" His voice stroked her ears making her tingle.

"Yes, thank you." Tension drained from her head and out of her body. The immediate effect surprised her.

"You're welcome." He replaced the contact with a soft kiss.

"Is that Kivronian medicine?" She tried to focus on something other than his mouth.

"It's an ancient technique. Most discomfort begins in the mind. We're taught early to control our thoughts." He wrapped his arms around her and nuzzled the top of her head. "Some thoughts require a great deal of discipline."

Pepper heard the smile in his voice and resisted putting her head on his chest. Her mind strayed to tasting his mouth, his heat and allure already addictive, but she couldn't succumb. She'd bared herself enough. Standing in his embrace felt too good and she shouldn't allow it, the danger obvious. She must protect herself.

In two days, Rafe had accomplished what no man since Josh had come near to. He'd elicited emotions that had been locked away for years. Could the binding be the cause? Vampires had skills humans knew nothing about. Could Rafe tear down her defenses with a word, a touch, or the brush of his hand? Her gut insisted he'd been honest. Sharing pain didn't make a relationship any more than a few alien words and a weird ritual, not to her. Given time, respect and friendship could blossom into love. She liked him. She cared, but time hadn't allowed for more. The man confused her heart and her head. She refused to deal with her body's response to him. *Traitor.* Take it slow.

# # #

The fire's warmth couldn't compete with the heat coursing through his veins. He wanted her. Strange, how removing her defenses opened him up. Protectiveness was innate to him, but what burned in his chest went beyond flesh to something he'd never encountered with other females, tenderness and a desire to understand this woman in his arms.

He'd never invested himself by divulging his past, had never considered it. Why would he? When his objective was sex, identifying with the target added complications. He'd persued his conquests, as he would battle. He'd relied on decisive action, combined with strategy, until he'd grasped his prize and had demanded unconditional surrender.

Women always gave in to him, often quicker than he'd like. He enjoyed the sex. But the chase, the skill employed to outwit and maneuver is what set his blood pumping. Easy victory deprived him of that rush. He needed a fight.

Pepper fought. Now, he understood why. He stroked her hair, indulging in the smoothness of the silky strands between his fingers. Overcoming her reticence to love would test his abilities as both a warrior and a man. If he had ample time, he'd talk with her, share strolls in the garden, and have dinner with her friends. He'd learn what she enjoyed and supply it, but time mattered. *I have twenty-eight nights.*

He was up to the challenge. He refused to be otherwise. He had to succeed. His sanity and Pepper's life depended on obtaining her love while reining in his lust for her. Under the best circumstances the latter would tax him. He wasn't operating at his best, not even close, but he could maintain control, shackling his feelings to silence the madness. What he felt had no bearing on securing her love. He'd gained the affections of many women without engaging his emotions.

Rafe ached for her and rubbed her lower back as she melted against him. And just when he felt her giving in, she stiffened and retreated into her fortress. He caught her fresh herbal scent and the arousal he'd hoped for. Pepper's flesh was willing, no matter her words and actions. When he began his seduction, she'd fall. He knew it. She wanted him more than she'd admit. There was no mistake. His Kivronian senses held fast, despite his illness.

They'd talked for a few minutes, each making clumsy conversation. Embarrassment scented her skin. That wouldn't help. One step ahead, two back. This slow process of winning her plucked at his patience like hairs pulled from his chest. Irritation was a problem, so was desire, and Pepper incited both. The binding should decrease madness. Were those only rumors tossed about to protect others like him? *I despise not knowing*

Take her. The voice slithered in his brain. *No.* Rafe's body tightened and he stamped down the prodding. He could survive under the weight of insanity, but not Pepper. While he'd suffer madness and disgrace if he claimed her body prior to the appointed time, being human, she'd pay the ultimate price. The fragile girl would whither and die inside. Insanity burning through her mind and spirit like Kivron's *Pool of Fire.* He had to protect her, even from himself.

Forcing his arms to drop from her enticing curves, Rafe stepped back. He cleared his throat. "It's late."

Her face flushed. "Um, yes." And Pepper retired to her room.

Rafe, burned with sexual tension, frustration, and insanity's murmurs resorted to other distractions. He needed physical activity and a way to work off the energy tensing his muscles. *Combat.* Sparring with Dante would take the edge off.

Pre-dawn light licked the tips of the pines and cast the patio in shades of gray. "That snake," growled Rafe, lunging with his Nova foil crossing weapons with Dante. "Garmood's found him."

The foils crackled. White sparks flew from contact. Dante pressed forward. "Garmood has his men in place. They guard Dr. Morgan constantly. He's under protection."

"Protection?" Rafe shifted his weight and pushed his brother back, the foil sizzling with heat. "No wonder, I've been unable to achieve her father's release." Rafe twisted his arm and the glowing foil grazed Dante's protective vest singeing the dusky fabric.

Dante's brows lowered. "Lucky."

"Skill," said Rafe, smiling and leapt away. Each took an attack stance, crouching and wary. They rounded like animals on the prowl sizing each other up.

Dante took a swipe at Rafe, the hot foil barely missing his arm. He jerked away. "Still quick, I see," said Dante.

"Agile enough to beat you." Rafe caught the tip of Dante's foil with his, their weapons humming with energy.

"Fast enough to take on Garmood?" Dante broke contact and crouched.

Sparring kept Rafe sharp. He enjoyed battle, the taste of victory and the surge of power from a fight. "I will be," said Rafe, searing the shoulder of Dante's vest before pulling back.

Dante glared at him, rubbed the smoking spot with his gloved fingers, and readied himself. "You'll never retrieve her father while Garmood lives."

Rafe engaged Dante's foil. "Not a problem." With a flick of his wrist, Rafe disarmed him, sending his brother's weapon sailing into the trees. "I'll dispatch the viper."

"Nicely done," said Dante, scanning in the direction of his foil.

They walked together to retrieve the weapon. The foil lay on a granite slab at the edge of a stand of quaking aspen, with their bright, golden leaves quivering in the breeze. Dante picked up the weapon and shut it down. The sun had risen above the mountains. Dawn painted sparse clouds with rosy hues touched with fire. The rays irritated Rafe's skin. He ignored the burning. Early morning hadn't always affected him. *The madness.* "Let's go in."

"Is it bearable?"

Rafe turned to find his brother's usually stoic face filled with concern. "It's bothersome. Less so since the binding." Rafe widened his stride to the house while keeping to the shade.

"I'm worried about Bram." Dante kicked a stone from the path. It hurtled over the flagstone walk and into the protection of boxwood.

"He has time."

"Does he?"

No one knew the answer to that, not even Bram. The course and speed of the Rosh madness couldn't be predicted. It was as individual as the males tortured by it. Rafe gave his brother the only answer he could. "He'll endure."

They walked in thoughtful silence, until they reached the house. Dante opened the French door to the dining room. "Bram's returned from Rome."

They entered. Rafe exhaled, tension released from his muscles as the burning to his skin abated. "Have you seen him?"

"Not yet. He's asked to report tonight." Dante received Rafe's foil and held out his hand for the protective vest.

Rafe pulled off the gear and handed it to his brother. Its weight seemed to increase since he'd buckled it over his chest an hour ago. Was there no end to the effects of this cursed illness? "Have Bram come after sunset. He can meet Pepper and we'll discuss negotiations for our sire's release." Fatigue hit Rafe with sudden ferocity. He steadied himself against the dining table. *This shouldn't occur. I'm bound.* Rafe willed himself to remain upright as energy fled his body. *Dante can't know. Not yet.* "You're excused."

Dante nodded, hefted the gear over his shoulder, and headed downstairs to the armory. Rafe stumbled and collapsed on the floor. His hands cushioned the blow of marble to his face. What was this? Insanity caused weakness, but it had never debilitated him. He lay prostrate on the ground, immobile. Only his chest moved with each breath and each required effort. *Unacceptable.*

Weakness would not be tolerated. *Get up.* He closed his eyes in concentration, visualizing power and energy flowing into his muscles. After endless moments, sufficient strength returned to allow him to kneel, a few more minutes and he pulled himself to his feet. The exertion dampened his crisp, white shirt. He refused to be overcome and dragged his body to the bar, hands trembling as he decanted a glass of blood. He gulped the ruby liquid. It slid down his throat, each swallow seeping into his tissues increasing vigor. *Thank the Kivronian deities.*

He'd fed before their bout. Did he require more? Had the mock battle or the exposure to the sun coupled with his illness left him vulnerable? He refilled his glass and drank. All believed madness increased a taste for blood, but the diabolical truth was *need.* How much human blood would he require to function?

People depended on him and the insurgency…. He shook his head. How dependable was he? Insanity no longer inched forward. It flew. At this rate, he'd soon be dangerous to others. How much opportunity remained to secure Pepper's love and to heal before he succumbed? *Like Hebric.* Rafe's heart twisted with a violent ache. He fought through the remembered massacre and loss. He refused to be beaten. Rafe finished the glass and dispensed another.

It might be weeks or days, but one night, physical weakness would lift along with the mental haze. He'd explode with potent force, his mind, keen and focused on death. He drained the glass without a breath. Tonight he'd meet with his brothers. He'd resist insanity's pull. But was it too early to discuss what must be done? If Rafe waited too long, he would end up like Hebric. He lowered his head. *No. That won't happen. I won't allow it.*

# # #

"I want to confirm my appointment with Lord Garmood," said Pepper, using the phone in her room. "Yes, this afternoon, thank you," said Pepper ending the call and laid down the phone.

Pepper fretted half the night over the emotional upheaval caused by Rafe's honesty and the sharing of her loss. By morning, she'd still lacked direction, except that she had to keep her appointment with Garmood. Rafe didn't like the dignitary, didn't trust him, and had warned her to be careful.

She'd make her own decision on the man. With her heart in jeopardy as Rafe tried to gain ground, she had to find out all she could. But could she trust either of them?

She had to get clear in her head where she stood in this odd relationship. Rafe strived to be good to her. Intuition whispered that he cared. The man was a dream come true by any woman's standards, but something niggled in her brain to be wary, and it was more than her fear of intimacy. This loomed dark. Was she so frightened that she invented monsters to push Rafe away? What did she want? She bit her bottom lip to distract from the knot forming in her center.

Loss had always been her defense, but the older she became, the thinner it wore. Until now, her reasons had shone threadbare. Pepper bent and tied her running shoes. Something scared her. Was it really Rafe? She stood and shrugged on a plum, fleece jacket over her tee shirt. No. She'd tried to make it about him.

The answer turned in her gut and moved into an ungainly knot. *It's me.* What would happen if she dropped her walls, took a risk, and maybe—loved him? Her heart raced and her head swam. She breathed through rising anxiety. *Why am I so damned afraid?*

She hadn't reacted this way with Josh, but then she'd been a child. That relationship had began with a young girls infatuation. Had she been in love with him or in love with the idea of love? After losing her mother, the world fell down around her, and she'd sought refuge in something normal. She'd hidden in the idea of love. The truth didn't sit well on her empty stomach, the knot swam in an acid sea.

Had she ever sustained a deep romantic relationship with any man? She hadn't had the tools with Josh. Did she possess them now? Her chest tightened. *That's it.* Rafe wanted a relationship, told her he did, and followed through. What if she ruined it? Pepper was terrified she'd fail or get hurt. She wiped her damp palms on her sweat pants. What if she bared her soul, if he learned everything about her wants, her fears, her human failings, and didn't want her? *Rejection.* What then?

If he couldn't love her, the misery would last until death, or longer if she accepted transformation. She couldn't survive a marriage where he glared at her over dinner, ignored her publicly, and despised her privately.

He's not that man, intuition argued with her. The man was perfection, strong, sophisticated, a leader among aliens. What was she? An average girl. Not a girl, a woman tired of loneliness. Her solitary existence might feel safe, but being entombed by fear wasn't living. Her thoughts shook her. Vampires weren't the living dead. *I am.*

An hour later, Pepper jogged through the wooded landscape of the sprawling grounds. Cool morning air, crystal blue sky, and the crunch of fall leaves accompanied her footsteps, their damp musty smell filling her nose as she pounded over the path. Wood-brown sparrows congregated in a granite birdbath ahead, then fled as she passed. Blackbirds whistled and called above, flitting from one pine bough to another, then landing to peck morsels found amid dry grass.

Running gave way to walking as she watched a squirrel, its cheeks bulging with forage. The fat rodent glared at her from the foot of a scruffy oak and chattered in anger before scampering up the trunk. The leaves had turned shades of copper, crimson, and brown in autumn's chill.

Foliage grew dense the further she walked, creating a heavy, multi-colored canopy. Unlike the pruned and planted European gardens adjacent to the mansion, this area remained natural. She preferred the wild, untamed growth. It stretched and sprouted, free of outward influence. Each tree, clump of sage, and shrub, unique and beautifully imperfect.

An uproar of magpies captured her attention. More than a dozen of the black and white scavengers moved over the ground near a wild currant bush, Its leaves partly summer green, partly a thrash of yellow gold. They squawked and pecked. What animal had died? Not a rabbit. Something larger lay beneath the undulating carpet of birds. Morbid curiosity propelled her feet. The cocky magpies screeched shrill warnings, but continued tearing at some unfortunate creature. No doubt a raccoon.

"Shoo! Get away." She yelled at the clamor and waved her arms, dispelling the raucous brood.

She blinked and blinked again. A few greedy foul lighted on their prize. Pepper ran them off. *It can't be.* The unwelcome, yet familiar sight of death overcame her doubt. She swallowed hard. Animals had done a good job of tearing and feeding. She realized that she wasn't looking at a furry woodland creature, but the body of a young woman.

"Oh, no," she murmured, and then gagged and spewed. The scavengers resumed their meal. Pepper turned away and wiped her sticky mouth on her sleeve. Her legs quivered from shock, adrenaline pouring into her limbs. What to do? *Run.* What if who or whatever did this watched? *Run.* Instinct screamed.

Her gut tightened. *Run where?* The body was on Rafe's property. He might be the killer. What if it were his somber faced brother, Dante? That seemed more likely and Rafe would protect him. *Oh, no. What to do?* Rafe held power in Red Rock. The only person above him was Garmood. Her head throbbed. *Run.* She turned and slammed into a wall of muscle.

Rafe stood before her, outfitted in the jet-black gear and helmet of an elite warrior. "What's wrong?"

"Rafe," she gasped, and stumbled back on shaky legs, trying to regain balance.

Dante appeared like a shadow dressed in his usual Enforcer uniform. She trembled. If Dante had murdered that woman, she could be next. Dante sniffed the air and moved to the mass of feeding birds. They scattered. "A human female."

Pepper chewed at her lip. There was little she could do. Too late to run, her best option was to calm down, and escape if needed. "I found her like that."

"Are you all right?" Rafe reached out to touch her.

She flinched, and he retracted his hand. "Shaken up is all." Plague had made her familiar with death. Corpses had lined the streets, awaiting bonfires to destroy disease. It wasn't the sight of a body, but of murder that dissolved her courage into tremors. She had to maintain her wits.

# # #

Rafe captured Pepper's hand, needing the contact to be sure of her and to calm himself. He scanned her, senses honed to detect injury. He found none. Pepper was safe. Relief untangled knots in his shoulders and allowed his lungs to breathe in air. His reaction startled him.

Dante hunkered down beside the lump of flesh. "A young woman, violated and ripped apart by purposeful violence."

Rafe's stomach churned as visions of carnage strewn across arid ground brought the bitter taste of bile into his throat and stirred up memories of his sisters. He tamped down his emotions. The torn flesh, and sticky blood, gone brown, the face contorted in horror were specters haunting his mind. They never left, but only hid in the cavern of his guilt. *If I'd been there, then perhaps....*

He yanked himself free of the past and focused on the situation before him. *It could have been Pepper.* The thought crushed his chest. Pain threatened to cut his heart from his body and hold it up to his face. When did he grow to care for her? Rafe shook his head. *I do more than care.* Was this love? It must be or the madness had found a new way to torment him. Feelings complicated the situation, but he gladly accepted them as a sign of a happy existence with her, if they survived. "What else have you uncovered?"

"The human female was murdered and dumped here," said Dante, in a stilted voice. "She's covered in blood, but little soils the ground. You see here." He motioned to the dry pine needles around her naked body. "The perpetrator was strong, definitely the work of a Kivronian male." Dante indicated the slashes over her throat, the jagged hole over her left side, and the rust-colored smears on her hips and thighs. Pepper covered her face with one hand.

"Could be madness," said Dante.

"Or, made to appear that way." Rafe's jaw tightened and his anger burned.

Dante stood and brushed off his hands. "Possible."

"Do you recognize her?" Pepper murmured, removing her hand from her eyes and glancing at the corpse.

Dante shook his head. Rafe wished he didn't recall the raven-haired woman. "She's the French Ambassador's daughter."

"You know her?" Pepper's eyes grew round and he

detected a spike in her fear.

"Publicly," Rafe assured.

"Would anyone connect you two?" Dante stalked around the woman, scanning as he went, each pass raising the scent of blood.

"I'm sure that's the intention," said Rafe. "Why else would the body be left here?" Pepper's hand chilled in his. Did she believe he'd done this? *Silch.* That would destroy her trust.

Dante's eyes darkened to obsidian and he rubbed his chin. "Garmood?"

"No doubt." The scent of blood piqued Rafe's hunger. Need made his mouth water and insanity pushed him to feed. *Not now*, he railed against his mind. "This murder will stir up human insurgents and threats of riot already exist. No one, but Garmood would incite chaos to lay hands on me."

Pepper's face went white. She shouldn't be part of this. He'd hoped to protect her as he'd tried to protect his sisters. *What a colossal failure.* He dragged his hand through his hair. *Not this time.* "You shouldn't see this. I'll take you to the house."

"No. I'm all right, really. You help Dante figure this out and I'll run to the house. I'll be fine," she answered too quickly.

Her eyes darted to the lump on the ground as Dante chased off the birds. "Um, I've seen death before. I can take care of myself. Besides, I'd rather be alone for a while."

The reek of fear surrounded her and slid from her skin like scales. He leveled his gaze on her face. "No."

Pepper fidgeted with the hem of her jacket. "The murderer might get away."

"The murderer may already be gone, and if not, I refuse to allow you to wander the wood as easy prey."

She froze. "You think he's still here?"

"It's not worth the risk. Either you leave with me or stay here where I know you're safe."

She stuffed her fists into the pockets of her jacket. "Fine. It's ridiculous, but have it your way."

"I will."

CHAPTER EIGHT

Pepper had seen death, its glassy stare, and shades of blue and gray pallor beneath skin. Bonfires exuding the stench of decay and acrid smoke were common during the plague. She shivered, amazed how the memory brought the rank odor to her nose.

The woman, lying a few yards away, hadn't died by indiscriminate illness. Raging fever and wasting disease hadn't eaten away her flesh leaving skin stretched over bone. Pepper closed her eyes to shut out the view. It didn't help. Visions of black hair matted with blood and a horror filled face invaded. Someone had stolen life. It could have been an animal. A mountain lion had the strength and teeth to do the damage she'd seen. But it hadn't. A more lethal creature had ripped her insides, left claw marks and blood clotted between her legs. Pepper's knees shook, and she hunched on the cold ground, resting her back against the rough bark of a pine.

With the world at the mercy of aliens, the likelihood rested there. Rafe blamed Garmood. The vampires would never hunt one of their own over the loss of a human. They might put out a notice for the girl as people did when searching for a missing pet, but nothing more would be done. Based on her own experience, humans held little value to an alien.

Pepper shifted her weight against the hard dirt and pine needles. Dampness soaked through her sweat pants and into her bones. Or was it the icy feel of death close by? Not just death, but murder. Who'd done such a vicious act? Was it Garmood, Dante, or could Rafe be the culprit?

With a touch, she could know. She only needed to take Rafe's hand or brush his side, and then ask a question. All his thoughts would pour from him into her mind. At least, that's how it seemed to work. The truth could be hers, if she had the courage to find out. How brave was she? "It's freezing. I'm ready to go with you."

Rafe stood under the shade of an elm and rubbed his eyes. "Wise choice."

She'd debated the wisdom of her actions ever since she'd met Rafe. Was he capable of such a disgusting and hateful deed? She hurried alongside this dangerous man, power leashed, but visible in his fluid stride, and each move of limb and muscle. With her arms tight around her body as if the feeble barrier would protect her from the onslaught of a lion or bear, Pepper struggled to keep up with him. Was she out of her mind? Her father had warned her that her curiosity would get her into trouble one day. This could be that day. "Do you believe the murderer is still on the property?"

Alert and ever scanning as they progressed down the path, Rafe strode an arms breadth from her. "It's possible, but unlikely." There was a sudden rustle in a bush and Rafe froze. He thrust Pepper back, his body between her and unknown danger. A rabbit darted across the trail. It's furry white tail burrowed beneath the protection of a wild rose bush.

"Unlikely?" She tilted her face in question.

Rafe shrugged. "Caution is always wise."

Caution, not something she excelled in when her need to know took over. "You think Garmood killed her?"

"Yes." They continued the trek, Rafe's silent steps making her aware of his skill as a predator.

Pepper moved closer to Rafe, feeling the tension in his frame. He was lethal. She opened her mind, but only vague darkness entered in. Nothing useful. *Stop being a coward and make contact.* Unwrapping her arms, she forced them to her sides. "What does Garmood have against you?" Her arm brushed his as she purposely stumbled.

His mouth hardened to a line. " Nothing personally."

She listened hard, and a few words leaked through his defenses. But how to make sense of theft, guilt, and betrayal? Were those against Garmood or himself? She needed sustained contact. "Do you mind if I take your arm? I'm feeling a bit shaky."

He smiled, a look of calm amusement, and secured her to his side. "Better?"

"Yes, thank you." A wall of steel met her mental prodding as they made their way from the woods and through the gardens.

Rafe steered them to the edges of the path close to the trees. She felt his concern for her, his worry over the murder, but no violence. That didn't insure innocence. She tried again. "Could someone else have killed the woman?"

He jerked to a stop and stared down at her, one ebony brow raised. "Give me some credit. If I were guilty, do you believe I'd leave evidence here? Dante and I are vampires and exist on human blood, but we're not fools. I've seen this style before. It's Garmood."

Thoughts, feelings, and pictures floated into her mind like wispy clouds. *The truth.* Her shoulders relaxed and she exhaled. "I'm sorry, but I'm trained to ask questions, search for proof, and not take anything at face value. I try to leave my emotions out of what I see, but sometimes they intrude. Do you blame me?"

"No. I might do the same in your position."

When they reached the house, Pepper excused herself for a shower and change of clothes. She stuffed the plumb jogging suit into a plastic bag for washing. Would she ever be able to wear it again without that woman's body coming to mind? *Doubtful.* After finding the body, she cancelled her appointment with Garmood. Rafe believed to his core in Garmood's guilt. She couldn't find evidence against it, and decided to stand on the side of caution, resorting to safer means of investigation.

Pepper smoothed her jade-green sweater over the waist of her jeans and found Rafe seated in the dining room, a tumbler of blood in his hand. With all her dark thoughts, she craved light and reached for the switch on the wall.

"Don't."

At the moment, she needed to break free from the confines of the house. She needed light and normal human conversation. She needed to forget the blood. "I'm meeting friends from the newspaper for lunch."

Rafe's handsome face looked pale, his features were drawn. Aliens didn't succumb to disease. It must be worry that cast the shadows. He drained the ruby contents of his glass and set it on the highly polished table. She'd never seen him in anything but a suit or uniform. He made the tailored, black leather jacket and jeans look good. "I'll join you." He stood.

That wouldn't do. She needed time away from vampires and anything that reminded her of death. Her glance fell to the red stained glass. Lunch with Rafe wouldn't help. "You'd be bored. It's just girlfriends catching up."

"It sounds amusing."

"It'll be dull as dirt for you."

"Nothing is dull when you're involved." He smiled and moved to her side. "Are you trying to get rid of me?"

Her polite avoidance had failed, she went with the truth. "I need to do something human and escape what happened for a while."

"I understand, but I can't allow it."

"Can't or won't?"

He didn't answer, annoying her further. She crossed her arms over her chest. "What are you doing about the murder?"

"Don't worry over it." He placed his hands on her

shoulders and stared into her eyes. "It's taken care of."

"I don't want to worry about it. That's why I'm getting out of here."

"No."

How did he do that? In a word the man ended all debate. His decisive tone and dark gaze broached no argument, but there was more, an unnerving edge that flowed from him in threatening waves. Rafe's thoughts trickled into her mind, thirst, barely controlled hunger, and exhaustion. She threw up her emotional barriers in defense. How could he subjugate such debilitating need? Something was very wrong. "Are you all right?"

He bristled at her question and removed his hands from her shoulders. Rafe flashed his devastating smile. It still played. But now that she knew him and felt his struggles, she noticed the fatigue he tried to conceal. His brown eyes, less bright, the smile, less vibrant. He leaned his hip against the dining table. "I'm excellent."

"Really?"

"Why would I lie?"

"That's what I'm trying to figure out." Her inquisitive, reporter's mind had her ramped up. "You're not well."

"I'm in superb condition."

"Right." She moved to the bar, filled a glass with blood, and handed it to him. "Here. I get the impression you need this. If you want to get to know me, then tell me the truth."

He lowered himself onto his chair, never taking his eyes off her. "Nothing is wrong." He drained the glass.

Her intuition was spot on. The man was famished. "Fine. Have it your way. Nothing's wrong. More?" She nodded toward the empty vessel clutched in his hand.

He slid his tongue over his upper lip and handed her the glass. "Please."

Pepper took the glass and watched as the decanter poured thick, warm blood. It sickened her to see the crimson fluid rise and to smell its coppery odor. "If you won't tell me the truth, I'll have to poke around until I learn it myself."

# # #

Madness rode Rafe hard. He'd barely rested the last few nights and he needed to escape into the oblivion of sleep from insanity's downward spiral. Pepper had caught him at his worst. He lacked patience for conversation and had no intention of admitting weakness. She tried him with questions. A steady flow of blood aided, but didn't overcome the effects of illness. Madness sucked his strength, increased hunger, and the kill in the woods accentuated his need for blood. At least, he maintained his wits. "You want truth?"

Pepper handed him the glass and sat beside him. "Of course. I hate lies."

What truth could he give her? Not all, that was too disturbing to contemplate. He wouldn't burden her. He sipped the fluid and doled out what information he could.. "Garmood isn't what he seems."

"What is he?"

Another question. "You've surmised that we have history." He despised getting into his past, but to detour her from the madness, he'd endure it.

She leaned forward, her eyes bright-green with interest. "I know you suspect and distrust him."

"It goes far beyond distrust." He finished the blood and set the vessel on the table. "Garmood has sworn a vendetta against my family." *How much should he say?* She asked for the truth and he'd give her enough to warn her. "That monster is responsible for my mother's death." Rafe's throat tightened, making it difficult for him to speak. "He brutally killed my sisters. It's no secret that he intends to exterminate our entire clan." He watched her reaction and marshaled on, hoping she'd take the danger seriously. "No Nucretah is safe as long as Garmood lives, including you."

Her eyes widened, lips parted, and color fled her cheeks. "You think Garmood wants me dead?"

"I know he'll use you to destroy me, if he can. What form that takes, I'm working to decipher."

Thoughts paraded behind Pepper's eyes. "You believe he murdered that woman, to get revenge?"

"Yes."

"Why? What started this feud?"

"My sire." Rafe shook his weary head. "Cadder took my mother from Garmood. It was legal, but he refused to accept it."

"What? I thought binding lasted forever."

"It does, unless during the betrothal period, the female chooses another. It's complicated."

Pepper raised her hand to stop him. "Wait a minute. Your mother was bound to Garmood?"

"Until she left him for my sire."

Pepper stared at the soiled glass on the table. "And this is why he's determined to kill all of you—and me." Her voice was thin, just above a whisper. "He did other things to that woman, didn't he." It wasn't a question. Pepper's voice trailed off. She trembled, pulled her legs up to her chest, and encased them with her arms. She reeked of fear. "You think Garmood intends the same for me." She rested her forehead on her knees and closed her eyes.

His stomach churned. The conversation brought back memories long ago exiled to the recesses of his brain. That monster thirsted for their destruction. If Garmood was responsible, the woman's murder had been a message, a vicious taunt designed to mimic the butchery of Rafe's sisters. He put his arm around Pepper's shoulder and pulled her close. She didn't resist. What could he say? To confirm her fears seemed cruel. She quivered against him like a leaf in the breeze. He couldn't lie. She'd stumbled upon the body and understood the danger. "I'll protect you."

Pepper leaned onto his shoulder. After a while, her quaking abated and she lifted her face to him with a weak smile. "If you're up to it, would you join me and a few friends for lunch?"

Holding her, feeling the weight and warmth of her body against him, Rafe almost felt whole. She'd handled the murder and news of threat better than he expected from a human. Her bravery astounded him. He planted a kiss on her brow. "I'd be honored."

# # #

A week had passed since Pepper had discovered the body in the woods. She refused to dwell on it and allow some monster to hold her hostage. Except for paying closer attention to her surroundings, and Rafe's constant watchfulness, she went about her normal activities. Each day, she minded Rafe's intrusion to her space less. Now, she awoke looking forward to spending time with him.

Pepper closed her eyes and soaked in the sun's warmth. A light breeze played over her hair and brought with it from a nearby orchard the sweet scent of ripe pomegranates. Rafe had promised her a surprise. She felt her lips curve into a smile. Every moment with Rafe was a surprise.

Usually, his power amazed her, traversing walls in search of clues to the killing, hurling spears with Dante at a target so distant she could barely see. It reminded her of the Kivronian games instituted last year. Similar to the old Olympic Games, but the losers suffered execution. Something about being unfit to be called Kivronian.

But there were moments, when out of the corner of her eye she caught him sagging against a wall. He'd appear exhausted and pale. Energy and strength gone, he struggled to maintain his cover of power. She knew it. With her intuition growing, she focused on him during those vulnerable times. He'd thwart her with his iron will and form a barrier difficult to pass, but a word or phrase would slip and embed itself in her mind, leaving her to creative pondering and conjecture. *Was he sick?* Vampires didn't get sick.

When she felt his fatigue, she offered him a glass of blood. He always accepted, always gulped the fluid as if he were starved for more. It worried her. He grasped at control. Within, she'd feel his anger flickering hot as jumbled mental images argued in his brain.

At first, it confused her. But after days with Rafe, she knew the distinct signature of his energy, and his mind. She felt him before he entered a room and heard his thoughts. It increased their connection. She understood more than a man like Rafe would easily admit.

He battled something inside that was so frightening, he needed huge amounts of energy to combat it. After one late-night conversation with him, she left the room to retire, but then returned to ask him something. She rounded the corner and stopped. Her gaze fell to Rafe, folded over on the floor. Beads of sweat dotted his skin. She wanted to run to him, but something in her mind held her back.

His thought floated into her head. *I can hang on, if only she doesn't see me like this. If she doesn't know my weakness.* Pepper chose to respect his wish and backed away. That's when she understood he struggled against things unseen, demons as powerful and corrupt as the creature that had murdered the unfortunate woman. Rafe suffered. It hurt her to know it.

For no apparent reason, some days seemed to try him. She felt it. His energy was siphoned off and confusion muddled his thoughts. It should have scared her, all that power wielded by a man at odds with himself, but it didn't. Rather, his stubborn need to hide his illness endeared him to her. And that did frighten her. Her compassion brought him close to her heart when nothing else could. Pepper knew Rafe had control, though *he* seemed to doubt. She felt his unwavering determination and strength to overcome what ever tormented him. It's who he was at his core.

Today was a good day. Pepper scowled at Rafe standing in the shade of a pine. "I don't like guns."

"Take it."

"Obstinate vampire," she grumbled, knowing he heard her. Pepper lifted the revolver gingerly. "Is it loaded?"

He chuckled. "Difficult to practice with an empty weapon."

The man was too charming, too gorgeous and right now, she wanted to hit him. "I don't see the point of this. Even if I learn to shoot this thing, what good will it do? A gun won't stop Garmood. Don't I need silver bullets?"

He smiled and her knees turned to jelly. "Not for practice. Legs apart. Both hands on the gun and hold it level. Don't jerk the trigger."

She rolled her eyes. "Are you finished giving orders?" She teased him, something she did often now.

He raised an imperious brow, not in annoyance, but playing with her. "Go ahead."

She lined up with her target, a row of tin cans on top of the rock wall twenty feet away. Sucking in her breath, she squeezed the trigger. The gun kicked. The explosion numbed her hearing. She missed the cans and hit a scruffy oak beyond. Bits of bark pulverized instantly.

"Nice shot." He tried to look stern, but the corners of his mouth twitched. "Again."

With her arms rigid, she stared at the can at her left and pulled a shot. It struck the lamp post above shattering the globe and sent shards bouncing to her intended target, toppling the can to the ground. "I'm improving. The can fell."

"Yes. That's one way to do it." Rafe adjusted her stance. "If Garmood stalks you, close won't be enough."

Rafe was right, of course. Close wouldn't save her life. It would get her killed. "One more time." She felt the weight of the revolver, the sleek, gray metal, and how it fit in her hand. She took her time focusing on the can of peaches in the center. Pepper squeezed off a shot. It ricocheted against the top of the wall below the can. *Damn, still not it.* She had to get it right.

"Try again."

She breathed in. Maybe she was over thinking it. *Relax.* She could do this. She glared at the offending peach can and squeezed the trigger. The bullet pinged the can and catapulted it into the air. "I did it," she squealed. "I can shoot." Exhilarated, Pepper practiced until her arms ached, and she could hit all the cans on Rafe's command.

"You'd make a decent soldier." Rafe took the revolver and kissed her cheek. "But you'll have to curtail jumping up and down each time you fell your target. It's not military." He grinned at her.

"I was celebrating."

"An admirable job. But I have my own ideas for celebrating." He stepped closer, his gaze smoldering with desire.

She knew that look, and had done her best to avoid falling prey to his appeal, but today she wanted his arms around her, and his mouth on hers. She licked her lips, anticipating his taste. It would be spicy like his scent, an addictive blend of cinnamon mixed with Rafe, making a heady aphrodisiac. The man was trouble. She knew it, but didn't want to avoid his touch. She longed for it. *It's just a kiss.*

His arms slid around her and with them came need, his or hers, maybe both. She didn't care. Pepper lifted her face waiting for his soft lips to take hers. His dark eyes focused on her as if burrowing into her soul, seeking a connection beyond flesh. It rattled her, but she held his gaze, amazed at her courage. Staring down a wild animal could be dangerous. Rafe was as instinctual a creature as she'd ever gotten close to—very close.

She breathed him in wanting to hold him there. *Just a kiss.* How could any man tempt with a smile, a curve of his mouth, a word? Everything about Rafe drew her to him, his humor in the way he teased, his determination to overcome weakness and do his duty, but most of all his tenderness. He could take her. The man was power personified. Yet he held off, something about the betrothal. He wanted to protect her. Did she want protection from his arms, his sultry mouth and heat of his body? *It's only a kiss.*

He lowered his head and brushed her lips with his. Warmth trickled down low in her belly. He teased by nuzzling beneath her ear, then kissed her neck. She moaned into the silk of his hair and leaned into him. She'd never felt so needy. *Kiss me.* Finally, he took her mouth, insistent and hungry. Her head fogged. She melted into him and a flame flickered in her core. His tongue stroked, prodded, and pleased beyond imagining. She wanted more. Slipping her hands beneath his crisp gray shirt, she caressed the velvet skin and hard muscle of his back. *I need.* Was that her thought? No, he needed her as much as she did him.

That moment of realization, where a kiss could turn into more, freed her from her amorous stupor back to reality. She pulled back. "I'm sorry. I need to go slow."

His mouth tightened and he breathed out in obvious

frustration.

# # #

How did she know? Rafe ran his hand through his hair. Pepper's ability to anticipate his needs astounded him. When his energy waned, she suggested they rest. If the sun prickled his skin, she asked to move inside. Always couched in terms of her need, not his. Two weeks since the binding, and they'd grown more comfortable with each other, but the ritual couldn't instill her degree of familiar knowledge of him. *This is different.* He had no means beyond his senses of determining her wants. And while he might discern she needed food, he didn't know what she'd prefer. His inability to read her thoughts challenged him. He paced waiting for her outside the women's dressing area of the clothing store, another first.

Her concern warmed him. Though he'd known many women, none had cared for him. They were out for what they could gain and gave no thought to him personally. *Until Pepper.* He smiled. How could one human woman lighten his heart and lessen his insanity?

Ridiculous. Yet, she did make a difference in how he felt. When with her, his mind cleared and his strength rallied. Thinking of her calmed the insidious voices. *Unusual.* He valued time with her. The many nights they gazed at the stars together as he pointed out constellations. He shook his head at his absurd actions. She'd convinced him to wish on a falling star. He didn't understand the human mythology behind a star hurtling through space to its demise, bringing good luck, but it pleased her when he took part and made a wish. All to please her.

He'd made a habit of giving her daisies, because she preferred those weeds above others, and it made her smile. She had a beautiful smile. He found her full bottom lip such a temptation, he had to look away to keep from kissing her senseless. It was lucky he found his mate attractive, but when her hair floated around her head like a cluster of stars, she stole his breath. He'd never experienced such a woman. Pepper had connected with him deeply. And it worried him.

As a black hole, her mind remained blank to him, but she might absorb thoughts. Could she walk through the chaos of his brain, see the madness, the drain from his abilities, and hear the murmur of violence? *Impossible.* Humans had no such ability. Even Kivronians couldn't rummage through each other's minds. *Ridiculous.* But if she did, what else had she learned? He kept dangerous secrets.

Pepper held up two gowns. "Which do you like, the green or the blue?"

Her question brought him back from his thoughts. He normally detested shopping, but with Pepper, he enjoyed it. She wanted him to choose. Could she read his thoughts? He'd test her ability. "You pick." *Choose Green. The green one.*

She grinned. "The green dress." Pepper handed the gown to the store clerk for delivery.

"It brings out your eyes." Not a definitive test, but possible.

"Thank you." She pecked his cheek. "I'm sorry I missed dinner with Bram the other night, but after... all that happened...." She shrugged. "I'm excited to meet him."

She'd found the body that day and Rafe thought it best they forgo the visit and secure the area. "Don't be. I doubt Bram will say much. He'd rather spend his time with available females." Rafe escorted her from the store, taking her hand, and enjoying the warmth and softness of her skin against his hard palm. Soon he'd enjoy more.

"Where to now?" She beamed at him. The street lights ignited flecks of gold in her hair.

"Across the street to my office. I've papers to sign. It won't take long."

"No problem. Who attends this pledge of loyalty?"

Rafe whisked her through the doors and into the elevator. He wanted Pepper to himself. "All warriors new to the quadrant and the usual dignitaries."

Pepper scrunched up her face. "Garmood?"

"Yes." Rafe punched in the floor number and the doors closed.

"I suppose it's a sign of disloyalty if I don't attend?"

"As my mate, it is."

She rolled her eyes. "Ugh."

"Don't worry." He smelled her concern. "I'd never allow anything to harm you."

Pepper took his arm. Her cheeks tinted that pink color he loved and her lips curved into a small smile. "It's strange, but even with a killer loose, I feel safer with you than I have in years."

He cleared his throat. "High praise." He hoped he lived up to it. *I'll defend you with my life.*

"I know," she said, and then looked quickly down. "I mean, you deserve praise."

Interesting. "For what, doing my duty as your mate? I'm bound to protect you." But duty didn't compel him. He'd offer his life out of love. *I love her.* The realization shook him.

She stared at him with wide eyes, and her mouth open, ready to speak. The elevator doors opened. Had she heard his thoughts? *Silch.* She must have. He didn't object to her knowing how he felt about her, but the rest. She shouldn't wade through the mire of insanity. It was dangerous. How could she view the violence and not fear or be affected? And the oath he'd taken, the secrets he'd sworn to guard. How much did she know?"

Pepper gazed at him, eyes shimmering. "You're a good man. You do what you must." Her voice quavered. "I…I'll stand by you."

Now what? Rafe towed her to his office. Was there any point in pretending? The girl apparently could pick his thoughts from his head as easily as he scented her worry. He'd never been much for avoidance, better to strike a target fast and sure. He escorted her into the room, then closed and locked the door. "What do you know and for how long?"

Her shoulders slumped as if a weight had fallen away. "So, I am picking up your thoughts. What a relief." She blew out a breath. "I believed I might be losing my mind at first, but then I figured it was the binding."

"Binding doesn't link us that way. What do you know?" He strode toward her, crowding her space.

She backed up against the bookcase. "I know there's something that hits you, sucks your strength, and affects your mind. I don't know exactly what it is."

A slew of Kivronian oaths fled his mouth. He didn't bother to keep them in his head. What was the point? She didn't know the name of his affliction, but she knew his symptoms. "What else?"

She stiffened. "I get pictures and bits of your thoughts. It's difficult to make sense of most of it."

"Try." He didn't want to be rough in his interrogation, but he had to gain every iota of information. His life, the lives of his brothers, and the rebels depended on what she knew. "What do you guess from your excursions in my mind?" Irritation building, anger flailing to be released, madness whispered— *betrayal. She can't live. Too great a risk.*

"I haven't told anyone and I won't. I recognize the risk to humanity. I am a reporter, but writing this story wouldn't help anyone, but the enemy. I'll keep your secrets." She lifted her chin in challenge. "You can trust me."

He trusted his brothers, but a human female? "Why did

you hide this from me?"

"I knew you didn't want me to know about your, um, weakness."

A stab to the heart. She knew. His fangs filled his mouth. *I have control.* "If Garmood learns I'm impaired, he'll act, and you've seen what he's capable of."

She nodded. "Is there a cure?"

He refused to think it. He would not share this, gain her pity and lose all. "What else have you gleaned from my mind? It's dangerous to learn too much."

Pepper rubbed her temples with her slender fingers. "Things flit into my head. I'm sure it's nothing. Just concerns over insurgents and your position."

"What?" He loomed over her. Don't think. Mind must be clear.

"Talon. The leader of the insurgents."

Rafe felt a cold blade at his throat, threatening to sever his head. He swallowed. "Do you know who Talon is?"

Her mouth trembled. "I'm not sure."

He grabbed her arms, his face inches from hers. "Who?" He growled. Desperation pushed him to act, but he quelled the need to wring it from her, and focused on hiding his thoughts.

"Tell me."

She pressed against the bookcase, unable to escape, fear shadowing her eyes, but still she refused to back down. "Let me go." She glared at him. He released his grip. Pepper rubbed her arms. "I don't know who Talon is, but you do."

CHAPTER NINE

Rafe glared at the container of blood perched on the dining table. He hadn't believed it possible, but Pepper's epiphany had ruined his appetite. He'd tired of refilling a glass and decided to use a brandy snifter, but his thoughts soured his stomach. How much did she know? She'd assured him, only vague impressions, a word here and there, and that nothing reliable came to her. Bits she pulled together and guessed at. She guessed too well.

They'd driven home in silence. If his thoughts came in pieces, then Pepper might skillfully work the puzzle until she knew everything. She was inquisitive by nature. Of course she'd keep at it. Her habit of questioning had both annoyed and amused him, until now. He grunted. He hadn't spoken and to protect vital information, he'd run Kivronian battle poetry through his head. By her quizzical look, she'd heard him. *What else had she heard?*

Since the binding, he'd spent countless hours with her. All that time she'd listened. Could she control her gift or did his thoughts bombard her like a meteor shower? He hoped she couldn't help it, that she wasn't acting the spy and slinking around his brain at will. She'd said as much. *Dare I risk it? What choice did he have? She was his mate.

He stalked from the dining room and outside to the secluded stone shed in the woods. His hands clenched, jaw tight enough to grind marble. Whatever she'd distilled from his mind, she knew too much. *Talon.* That name alone ensured his head on a pike and would wipe him from the annals. He swallowed the bitter thought along with the pain of Hebric's end. His efforts protecting the human rebels blown away like wind driving sand from rock, and it stung.

He raked his hand through his hair, pulling the strands tight. Was Pepper his salvation or his end? At the least, she put humanity's fight for freedom in jeopardy. She'd sworn she didn't know anything beyond his affiliation to the insurgents, that she'd never divulge his secret. He believed her. He could smell a lie and she'd meant her vow. He paced in front of the shed, his polished leather shoes crunching over brown pine needles. But in the skillful hands of a master like Garmood, strong Kivronians had buckled and spewed all they knew. Rafe trembled at the memory. His hand covered the jagged scar on his side. It only ached on occasion. She'd never survive such inducement.

A twig snapped. Rafe turned toward the sound and sniffed the air. "Come out Bram."

His brother crashed through scrub oak. Dry leaves stuck to his dark, wavy hair. He looked much like Rafe, but his demeanor was brash. He swaggered, was hot headed, and was so near one thousand years that Rafe worried when the madness would befall him. Bram grinned as he approached. "I see you're hearing remains sharp."

"I'd have to be deaf to miss you tromping through the forest." Rafe smiled. It warmed him to have Bram home, if only for a short time. Their closeness was born of respect and of Rafe's affection for the brother who'd rescued him from Garmood. "Where is Dante?"

Bram pulled a bramble from the sleeve of his battle suit. "Coming. What's this about?"

"We have a complication."

"Always something." Bram shrugged, accentuating the restraints of the uniform on his rebel nature.

Dante emerged through a stand of pines without so much as a rustle. "Perimeter's clear." He nodded to Rafe and Bram. "Dr. Morgan has boarded the transport. He'll arrive tonight.

You wouldn't believe what it cost and the favors we owe." He sighed heavily.

"It had to be done, no matter the expense." Rafe needed every tactic to gain Pepper's love. Securing Dr. Morgan was welcome news. Precious little of it. "Thank you. Dante, you'll meet the transport and bring Pepper's father to the house. I want him protected at all times." Rafe clasped his hands behind his back, steeled himself, and forged ahead. "Talon is compromised."

Dante's eyes narrowed. "How?"

"Who is it?" Bram calmly pulled a dagger from his belt "I'll eliminate him."

"No," Rafe blurted. "It's not that simple."

Bram smirked. "Oh, Kivronian elite."

Rafe twisted his mouth. A member of the High Council would be protected., but this was more complicated. He had to tell them. "It's Pepper. She's a black hole with the ability to read Kivronian thoughts. We can't move forward with the plan."

Bram and Dante stared, as if waiting for the punch line of a bad human joke. "You're serious?" said Bram.

"Yes. She swears she doesn't know who Talon is, but she

could happen upon it from any of us. One unguarded moment could fill her mind with Bram's secret identity." Muscles tightened between Rafe's shoulder blades. "She knows about the madness and no telling what else."

"She's a liability." Dante said simply, his face blank as stone. "If she weren't your mate, we'd have options. As is, we must protect her."

Rafe summoned his control. "I'm aware of the risk. I suggest the two of you stay clear of her. I'll take advantage of the human tradition of a honeymoon and take her on a trip."

"But we need you to run interference." Dante's stony mask crumbled around his mouth. "Over fifty humans are scheduled for transfer to the factory."

"I know what happens in that place. I've seen it," Rafe growled. Memories of frenzied human screams reverberated in his head and the stench of bowels released in terror filled his nose. Fatigue bombarded his body. He must remain in control.

"I won't stand by while the Council quietly drains the life from defenseless people." Bram rumbled. "And what they do to the bodies, the desecration of flesh. I can't abide the sight of that discount sludge the Council sells. If Kivronians knew how they came by it..."

"But they don't know," said Dante. "And without proof, no one would believe it. Those rebels sacrificed to help us. Jonah lost his mate in the explosion. The Council tortured Rachel. She'll never regain use of her legs. We can't ignore them."

Rafe breathed in the fresh pine air, hoping to drive the fog from his brain. "It's Bram's call. Don't inform me about your plans, not with Pepper absorbing my thoughts like a sponge, and Garmood looking for an opportunity to take me."

"You expect to be captured?" Dante's somber gaze darkened to pitch black.

"It's likely," said Rafe. "Garmood's ordered an investigation on the missing French woman. It's only a matter of time before he finds an excuse to arrest me."

Bram flexed his fingers. "Taking Pepper away only puts off the inevitable. That *crimwad* will never stop until he hunts you down."

Rafe's past assailed him, silver chains seared his skin, Garmood's vicious claws sliced deep. Sweat dampened his skin and he shook himself, dispelling the vision. "He's already begun. The murdered woman in the forest was a trap. If not for Pepper, it might have worked. Dante incinerated the body and cleaned the site, but we're all in danger as long as Garmood exists." Rafe leveled his gaze on his brothers. "He won't stop with me."

Bram shrugged one shoulder. "Then we'll have to squash the worm. I think he's lived too long already. Dante and I will devise a way to free the humans. You take your mate away from here. That might put Garmood off his game. Maybe he'll get sloppy and have an accident." A mischievous grin tugged up the corners of Bram's mouth. "Or disappear."

Rafe slid a sideways glance at Bram. "Don't think it. Garmood is too dangerous to tackle alone, even for someone with your abilities." Dante and Bram bowed their heads in obedience and Rafe embraced them, arms wrapped around broad shoulders. "Stay safe."

# # #

Dante left to prepare for Dr. Morgan's arrival. Rafe surveyed Bram spreading his weapons on top of a stone wall beside the shed. He checked each, as meticulous in his attention to his tools as he was to his women. Other than Garmood, what danger did he expect?

"Planning trouble?"

Bram looked up through dark strands of hair fallen over his right eye. He wore it long and tied back, but nothing could confine his thick waves or his boisterous personality for long. "Always."

"Any reason?"

"There's always a reason."

Rafe shook his head, resigned that danger followed his brother like a shadow. "With you there is. Trouble finds you. Don't start any while you're here."

Bram grinned and returned his weapons to his belt. "I don't start it, I finish it."

"Then don't finish anything."

Bram laughed, a husky chuckle that hid indiscretion and intent. "Ask no questions and I'll tell you no lies."

"You've never been able to lie to me."

"No need. I trust you."

A lump formed in Rafe's throat. Those words meant everything. "I need something from you."

Bram adjusted his Nova sword on his hip, but stopped to glare at Rafe. "I'm not lending you my new dimension booster."

"Not that." Rafe swallowed the discomfort, but the words still must be spoken.

"What?"

"It's the madness."

Bram waved off the words with his hand. "I'm fine. Don't worry about me."

Rafe doubted that, but he knew Bram would never admit weakness. How could he express his own bouts with insanity? How to ask this brother for a gift too terrible to utter? Bram stared at him. His dark eyes flecked with shards of gold near the pupils. Only Bram carried the unique trait, a combination of warmth and unfathomed depths.

Rafe breathed in, wishing he could ignore his situation, the madness growing inside him, the short time left to gain Pepper's love, and his responsibility to those he cared for. But he was made of stronger stuff. He couldn't shy away from honor. Duty pulsed through his veins. He had to act. "I trust you above any. It's why I must ask this of you."

Bram cocked his head. "So serious. What is it?"

Best to say it. Rafe cleared his throat, searching for his voice. "After I return with Pepper and the betrothal is complete, if I have failed....if you notice the illness gaining ground...don't wait."

"No." Bram bellowed. "I won't. How can you ask me?" Bram closed the distance between them, eyes glistening with emotion as he leveled his gaze. "You're part of me."

Rafe tightened his jaw, fighting against a tremor. "That's why I must ask. You'll recognize when I'm close, you'll know when I'm past safety and near violence. There's no one else I can trust."

Bram lowered his head, thick black hair shielding his face. His shoulders sagged. "Rafe." He whispered the choked plea.

It broke Rafe's heart, but he couldn't show weakness, not now, not in this moment. Here he must remain strong and elicit Bram's promise. Emotions crushed his chest, his eyes burned, but he wouldn't falter. "It must be you. Dante won't be aware in time. I'll annihilate him and Pepper. So many will die. If the moment comes, I need you to end me. For all our sakes."

Bram threw his arms around his brother, pulling him close in a hard grip. "As you will."

# # #

She didn't know where Rafe went, and right now, she didn't care. *Irritating, close-minded man.* He knew her secret and she knew his. He'd hardly listened when she'd tried to explain how it worked, that she hadn't tried to delve into his private matters. Things just came.

Once they were dumped into her head, she worked to

make sense of them. It wasn't her fault she absorbed aliens' thoughts. *It's not as if I asked for this--gift.* How long could he remain angry? She hadn't set out to compromise his position and ruin him. How was she to know he had connections to Talon, enemy number one of Kivronian rule?

Pepper trudged downstairs, her sneakers thudding on the carpet. She needed to vent her frustration and target practice sounded like a perfect diversion. The armory walls were loaded with weaponry from rocket launchers to grenades, and from Kivronian Nova swords to Neutron eliminators. The array spoke to the aliens' need for military supremacy.

Rafe enjoyed guns and swords, but his favorite was displayed on the far wall, an old-fashioned bow of sleek metal paired with a quiver of steel arrows. Their entire culture centered on battle, closely followed by perfection, power, and clan loyalty.

Rafe certainly had the role of clan Alpha. She moved to the bow and stroked the graceful curve, lethal in the right hands. Alphas relied on strength to maintain position. Was Rafe angry because she'd uncovered his vulnerability? It made sense. Her fingers ran over the steel shaft of an arrow. Rafe wielded the weapon with precision and ease. It required strength and a keen eye, neither of which she possessed. Rafe had lifted the bow, held it steady, and savaged an apple so far away it appeared a dot on the tree stump in the woods. He made it look easy, as he did everything unless his energy failed.

Wild dogs would attack and kill an injured pack member. Would aliens execute Rafe for illness? She pursed her lips and stared at the bow. Kivronians possessed no patience for weakness. Losers in their games met swift death. *Unfit.* Her stomach sank. No wonder Rafe fought to hide his struggle.

To look at the bow, she wouldn't think flexibility played a part, a perfect balance of rigidity and give to unleash deadly force. Too much tension ruined the bow, not enough and the arrow fell short. Pepper stepped back and surveyed the store of implements designed to kill. They represented Rafe's need for control and protection. And that he'd been trained to think and act, always vigilant, and superior. Could he be otherwise? Alien culture ran deep and he couldn't help who he was, it embedded his genes. He had to fight. No, it was more than that. He had to win.

Rafe ran the Western Quadrant, ruled his family, struggled with illness, fought for human freedom, and dealt with Garmood. *And I've added to his burden.* How much tension could he withstand before he snapped? How did he juggle everything with control, elegance, and his knee-weakening smile? Somehow, he did. Her anger dissolved under the flood of Rafe's responsibilities, and her own selfishness. He amazed her. Not just his strength, but also his compassion for her people. She'd never known a better man.

Her breath stilled in her chest. Another man held a place of respect and love in her heart. Her father. He'd worked to save people from plague. While Rafe and her father fought and struggled differently, both had done so for the benefit of humanity. But Rafe sacrificed all. A chill shimmied up her back. His discovery would guarantee his execution.

Her chest constricted at the thought. *Rafe gone.* When they'd met, she'd felt attraction. Who wouldn't? But this went beyond, more than his smile that melted her insides, more than his voice weakening her knees with one word, more than his devastatingly handsome persona. He'd touched her heart. *Damn.* She respected his courage and self-sacrifice. What she felt didn't sprout from lofty ideals—not alone. How had Rafe gotten inside?

His thoughts.

She read his mind and felt his emotions. She knew his past,

his hurts, fears and dreams. He wanted children and a home. He wanted her. She knew him, and familiarity brought affection and an intimate connection she never would have allowed on her own. Rafe relied on a façade of power and control. She saw through it. The vulnerable man suffering, yet carrying on without complaint. Rafe pushed through to serve his people and save humanity. To save her.

She could see herself in his arms, kissing him, wanting his touch. She fantasized a happy marriage, having a home and children with him. And love, someday in the future, but not if he got himself killed. Rafe needed her help.

He'd never ask for assistance and he'd refuse if she offered it. *Stubborn alien.* She resolved to ease his load. But what could she do beyond keeping his secret? Not much different than protecting a source. She could utilize her skills and ferret out information for Rafe. *I'm a black hole. Why not make use of that?* He'd object. He'd argue the danger, and glare at her with his compelling eyes, and then quietly tell her no. This time, it wouldn't work. She was determined.

Pepper lifted the revolver, grabbed a box of ammunition, and headed for the stairs. She could take care of herself. Surviving chaos and violence during the plague counted for something. Adversity taught her to pay attention to facts and honed her intuition. Her gut had saved her life more than once. It would save her now.

But more than survival, her original desire to work as a journalist was rooted in a fierce need to make a difference. Her longing to uncover the truth, to sever the lies that kept a collar around humanity's neck, pushed her to delve into Rafe's mind. Life had plopped an opportunity at her feet. Excitement prickled her skin and she jogged up the remaining stairs. Better than writing about the insurgents' battle for freedom, she'd join the fight.

CHAPTER TEN

There was no reason to shield Pepper from the truth. She knew. Rafe slid travel brochures into the yellow envelope and pushed back against the soft leather of his chair. His home office had been his refuge from the incessant perfection he portrayed outside these walls. *No more*. No hiding behind his impeccable façade, his control, or position. Pepper knew. The truth delivered itself to her mind. Now he realized how humans felt and he didn't much care for the experience.

Telling her romance motivated the trip wouldn't cover the danger of staying in Red Rock. He shook his head. Who was he kidding? She understood the peril. If finding the body hadn't convinced her, then delving through his brain must have. *Silch.* She might have come upon the memory of finding his sisters, even his torture. He swallowed hard. She must be terrified. The truth carried some advantages. She wouldn't argue over leaving town.

He tossed the envelope on his desk, leaned his head back against the chair, and closed his eyes. How did he feel about anyone seeing all that he was, his fears, intimately connected to his weakness, his desires, and his failures? *I despise it. She'll never love me now.* How could she? Pepper saw beneath his careful political mask to the total man. Even the parts, he denied to himself. If he refused to accept his flaws, how could she accept them? No woman wanted a mate that lacked. *Lacked? I'm inching toward deranged.*

Disappointment twisted his gut. For the first time in his long existence, he loved a woman, and had been lucky enough to bind her, but because of fate's cruelty, she'd never return his affection. Caring wouldn't save him. She'd have to be insane herself to love him, now that she knew the darkness inside him. Madness hadn't destroyed him, not yet, but it would.

Like a bolt of lightening illuminating his mind and burning a hole in his chest, realization hit him. He sat upright, his eyes wide. *I have no control. None.* Nothing he could do or say would alter the truth. She knew everything or would, the madness, the lies he told himself, and the truth he hid from.

He sucked in a breath forcing the air into compressed lungs. *Consummation.* She'd hesitated before, now she might spurn him. He'd never force her, but after the betrothal they must consummate to seal the binding and to stop his slide into destruction. His jaw tightened. He couldn't read her mind, but knew her well enough to suspect that she'd take him to her bed out of the most loathsome reason imaginable, pity. No woman had ever pitied him, but he saw pity in Pepper's gaze when he trembled with fatigue. He caught glimpses of her concern when his patience wore thin. "Pity." The word lay like mud in his mouth.

Reality proved worse than the nightmare of madness. Insanity's murmurs couldn't compete with the truth, more vile, more painful and destructive than even Garmood's torture. That had ended. Pepper was his for eternity, unless she refused him. He leaned over the desk and rested his head in his hands. She won't refuse. She'd read his mind and knew the price they'd pay for failing to complete the binding with consummation, madness unleashed on an unsuspecting world, like Hebric. Fear, pity, duty, out of these she'd have him, but not out of love.

Rafe snatched the envelope, and strode from his office, sickened by his thoughts, and the reality that soured his stomach. He shoved away anguish and dwelled on his love for Pepper. How he anticipated her touch, enjoyed being with her, and her mischievous grin that brightened her eyes when she teased him. If she read his mind, at least when they did make love, she wouldn't doubt his sincerity.

He came upon her in the hall, hair askew, copper strands floating about her head like feathers in a breeze. Dressed in a baggy sweatshirt and jeans, she enticed him. "I've a surprise." He held out the envelope and focused on her full lips. How he wanted to kiss her.

Her face tinted pink. She accepted the envelope and pulled out its contents. "A trip?" She shuffled through the brochures. "Which one?"

"All of them. I thought we'd take an extended honeymoon. Spain, Italy, Moscow, India."

Her brow crinkled. "When do we leave?"

"Tonight, after the pledges of loyalty."

"Why so soon? The betrothal isn't finished and you said we couldn't, well, it's too early for a honeymoon." Color spread from her face down her neck.

"Then call it a vacation."

"How long?"

Long enough. "We'll return to complete the betrothal and then continue our trip."

She twisted a thick strand of hair around her fingers "It's Garmood. What's going on?"

"It's wise if we leave for a while. Why not enjoy it?"

"Safer?"

"Yes."

"We can't run forever."

"We won't." He smiled, trying to win her over while guarding his thoughts. "This is strategy."

"Then you have a plan?"

"No."

"Stop being cryptic. You know sooner or later it will seep into my head. Someone has a plan and you hope it's over before we return." She shoved the brochures back at him and he took them. "You believe I'm dangerous and want me out of here."

"Not you, but your ability."

She crossed her arms over her chest and scowled. "Sorry, it's a packaged deal. Can't separate the two. If I could, I would."

"Darling, you know my thoughts. I want you safe, and yes, there is danger because of your ability. Leaving is the best way I know to protect you."

"You mean it's the best way to protect everyone else from what's in my head. I'm a liability. Don't you think I know that?

You don't trust me."

"I don't trust Garmood. You've seen what he's capable of."

"Yes." Her mouth twisted in disgust. "What's the other surprise?"

"Nothing. And stay out of my mind. Don't you have any control of what you pick up?"

"Some, but I have to concentrate."

"Then concentrate on blocking my thoughts. Most aren't fit for human consumption and certainly not your's."

# # #

Before she could stop them, visions of Garmood's butchery violated Pepper's brain. *Monster. Creature. Assassin.* Names synonymous with the dignitary thirsting for their blood filled Rafe's mind and fled into hers. She concentrated and revoked the twisted images. How did Rafe appear calm when memories of torture and loss lurked around every corner of his mind? Garmood was a grotesque beast. She swayed from the vile onslaught.

Rafe pulled her into the strength and safety of his arms. His spicy scent calmed her. The warmth of his body heated her. Comfort wrapped around her and she felt as if they'd known each other forever. *I've changed.* They'd connected and she could admit her need for his companionship and love. Not that she loved him, not yet, but every day brought her nearer to throwing off her armor.

Rafe's thoughts careened into her head. She couldn't stop them and trembled from the force. *Madness. Destruction. Lacking.* She pieced together the morass of words. *Pity.* She focused and formed coherent meaning. *She'll never love me.*

How could he think she'd never love him? Rafe was beyond lovable, even if she struggled with her heart, he deserved her love. She lifted her head and caught the sadness and need in his gaze. His ache and longing ran into her, and took hold, bringing tears to her eyes. How could he bear his pain and loneliness?

No matter the risk to her emotions, she couldn't allow him to believe a lie. She blinked away moisture. Anxiety replaced sorrow and steeled her resolve. *I will do this.* She bravely met his gaze. "Rafe," she squeaked.

He cocked his head. "Yes?"

"I, um…"

He continued to stare at her, expectant and wanting. She breathed in and then out, slowly working to form her thoughts into something sensible. "You're wrong."

"Really?" One ebony brow lifted.

It was more difficult than she'd imagined. She used words for a living. *Get over it. I'm going to do this.* "I respect you. I'm in awe of your strength, your courage, and your compassion."

"Are you?" His mouth twitched.

"Yes." Once she got going, her feelings gave way. "You're the most amazing man I've ever met." She sucked in air along with courage. "I care for you. It's too soon to call it love, but it's moving in that direction."

He gazed at her, speculating. "You could love me? Even with knowing...." His voice trailed off.

"The madness?"

He flinched. "Yes."

"I'm concerned for you, but not frightened. And I don't pity you. Why would I think less of you because you have something to overcome? You're more than capable."

"It's not entirely up to me."

Before she could complete the question in her mind, the answer came. *You are. Your love is key.* The one thing he needed from her and she feared to give it. "I want to love you." *Oh, did I say that out loud?* Mortified, she lowered her head and stared at her shoes.

"Pepper." He gently lifted her face with his fingers, forcing her to meet his hopeful gaze. "You can accept me as I am, everything?"

She wanted to. "I know who you are. I see into your mind and watch you battle everyday. I accept you, Rafe, as much as I'm able."

He slid his hand behind her head and captured her mouth with his in a demand bordering on desperation. His tongue caressed the interior of her mouth and she was lost in his kiss, taking, wanting, and needing with a fierceness that rivaled his thoughts. She jerked his crisp, gray shirt free of his slacks, and caressed his chest, rough hair brushing against her palms. He deepened the kiss and pressed her tight against him. He wanted her. But she didn't need to read his thoughts to know that.

It had been so long since she'd made love. She felt awkward, but starved for affection and for a man's touch. *No, Rafe's touch.* He released her mouth and nuzzled the sensitive spot on her neck just below her ear. She moaned. The delicious scent of his hair proved a powerful aphrodisiac.

He shifted her baggy sweatshirt. The gun and box of shells she'd hidden there escape from her pockets, crashed to the floor, and rattled over the tile. Rafe stared hungry-eyed at her. "Protection? Not from me." His tongue took a slow, seductive swipe over his lips.

Her knees wobbled. All that he wanted to do to her washed through her mind and into her body, filling her core until it pulsed. She'd never felt this, not with any man, the yearning and searing need that went beyond flesh down to bone. She'd have him here in the hall right now. Her fingers moved to his slacks and pulled at his belt. He grabbed her hand. She whimpered. "Please," she breathed. Her body sizzled with desire. He had to smell her need and the taste of it on her skin.

"Shh. Don't tempt me. We mustn't." He brushed his lips over hers. "Soon, darling." He kissed her, soft gentle brushes over her face.

"It's that damned betrothal," she groaned.

He chuckled, drawing her close, his fingers splayed over her back. "My thoughts exactly."

# # #

Rafe drove to the government complex speculating over the delights of making love with Pepper. For the first time in weeks, he dared hope for his future. She admitted tender feelings that could cure him. She'd come far in two weeks. In two more, the betrothal ended and he'd claim Pepper's heart as well as her body. The dismal voices assailing his mind were thwarted by her brave words. He knew it cost her. Letting down her guard had frightened her and still she'd overcome fear to express her feelings. It made him love her more.

The taste of her clung to his lips and fed his want, but desire could undo everything. If he pushed, she would give in to seduction. She'd come close, her scent filled with lust, her body begging for his. In a weak moment, he'd take her. Having Dr. Morgan as a chaperone would curb him. If madness flared, Rafe would control the whispers, the urges for violence, and need for sex. *I can endure anything for two more weeks.*

Pepper's passion had lifted his mind from the doldrums. They'd travel Earth. With no sector to run and no enemy fixated on their demise, Rafe would gain her love. He felt giddy at the prospect. Peace, sanity, and someone to share it with. *Not someone, Pepper.* He strode through the lobby of the government offices, nodding to the receptionist and Enforcers patrolling the building. Perhaps she loved him, but didn't realize it yet? Would that make a difference to his cure? He opened his office door and stepped inside. *Two weeks.* He'd know soon enough.

Hours crawled by, but he had to maintain normal

operations. Not even Celeste knew he planned to leave. He'd kept his schedule and Dr. Morgan's visit secret. Success required stealth. Rafe parted the thick, russet draperies and glanced at the sky. The sun sat like a ball of yellow fire over the mountains on its path toward night. He watched as it sank behind jagged peaks, silhouetting black against gold.

Darkness comforted him. Was it diminishing light or the mending of his mind that brought solace? The cure of the Rosh madness was so close he could taste it. Taking blood from her again would finish the betrothal, and if she loved him, he'd be whole. *I am improving, I'm certain of it.* Things were working out perfectly.

Celeste cleared her throat and Rafe closed the curtain. She stared at him, thin, efficient, and cold as the early snow dusting the mountain peaks. "Lord Nucretah, sorry to disturb you, but there's an urgent communication from Kivron."

He didn't have time for complications. "What is it?'

Her silver eyes shimmered. "Allow me to read it."

"Very well."

"To Lord Rafe Nucretah, General of the Fifth Army, defender of...."

"Dispense with that and get to the message," Rafe

interrupted.

Celeste scrolled down the screen of her Intel device. "Here it is. You've been awarded a Kivronian female in the Lottery."

Impossible. He couldn't have heard right. "But I'm bound."

"Not quite. The betrothal's not over. This states all previous contracts regarding a human mate are voided." Celeste smiled, her thin red lips stretched over prominent white teeth. "Congratulations."

Rafe's head swam. A few weeks ago he would've accepted the news with joy, but now…. "I decline."

Her mouth gaped. "You can't defy the Council. This is a great honor. You've been chosen to receive a mate who can produce children, ensure your family's future, and propel you to serve on the Council."

"If it's not a direct order, I will forgo."

Celeste's eyes hardened to steely balls. "It is an order, not that you should need to be compelled to take this gift. You can't give up everything for that—human."

Rafe growled. "That *human* is my mate. Her name is Pepper. And I warn you, speak of her with respect."

Celeste's thin body stiffened as a dry reed. "You're ordered to release Pepper and report to Kivron as soon as possible,

Lord Rafe."

"It's too late."

"For what? Do you feel something for the girl? You'll get over it." She put her bony hand on his jacket sleeve. "Once you're bound to your true mate, all ties to Pepper will dissolve."

He glared at her in warning. "I don't want them dissolved."

She softened her tone. "Rafe, it's for the best. You'll elevate your family, be beyond Garmood's reach, and give your brothers higher priority in the Lottery. You can't mean to deny them the opportunity because of a girl. Refusal will ruin you. It's insane."

Everything Celeste said was true. His brothers would benefit. He'd gain prominence and the family he longed for, but giving up Pepper was unthinkable.

CHAPTER ELEVEN

Avoidance wasn't his style. Rafe pulled his charcoal gray dress uniform from the bedroom closet. He had to think things through. How would he tell Pepper of the Lottery? He wouldn't trouble her, except she'd pick it up from his mind when she laid eyes on him. Then he'd be dealing with damage control. He despised taking the defensive. It would be better to attack the situation head on. He'd inform her there'd been an error. A trifle, just a technicality.

She'd trust him to take care of the situation. *Trust.* Not something that came easy to her. But he'd made inroads. She'd let down her defenses, accepted his affection, and admitted she cared. He hoped that was enough. Human females were jealous creatures.

He donned his jacket and hung the medal for bravery about his neck. The ruby-jeweled Kivronian animal resembled a bat and fed on blood. *Dragoste* savagely fought to the death in defense of mate and young, a fitting symbol of courage and sacrifice. How much sacrifice must he endure? First war and capture, then transfer to Earth, and now, perhaps the one thing he valued most, Pepper. Even if the odds were in his favor that he might gain a Kivronian mate, and children, he couldn't pay the price of losing the woman he loved. The cost was too high.

He refused to pay it. Finding love on Earth with a human was rare. No male sought such a relationship, unless the Rosh madness forced him. Obligation and position took precedence. The binding connected well enough—in most cases. His relationship with Pepper went beyond obligation. He couldn't lose her. A reasonable discussion with the Council would solve the issue of the Lottery. Rafe tugged on his jacket sleeve. He had no intention of binding himself to anyone else. Children or not, he wanted Pepper.

Besides, the Council wouldn't award a Kivronian female to a man aleady betrothed to a human, not with so many males desperate for a mate. What cast off were they trying to dump in his lap? Perhaps, one of Liptar's unfortunate daughters. Rafe shuddered. All six were scraggly excuses for Kivronian females. He couldn't bear the thought of mating with any one of them and swallowed distaste. They made Celeste appear a goddess.

All women paled compared with Pepper's beguiling beauty, but her unique ability to tease him, and care for his needs without drawing attention to his illness made her a prize. With her, joy bubbled up into laughter. His mouth spread into a smile. And the way her hair exploded around her head in shades of copper, auburn, and gold like a newly formed galaxy, made him ache to touch the soft curls, kiss her lips, and work his way down to the rest.

Rafe adjusted his collar and tied the white silk about his neck. Who'd bent the Lottery rules? They had to be working with Garmood, whose devious stench permeated this odd turn. This was no mistake, but another trap. What did the monster hope to gain?

Rafe entertained scenarios. If he refused the win outright, he'd incur the Council's wrath, be stripped of rank, position, and property. His brothers would suffer by association, outcasts all. Garmood would enjoy that outcome. Reduced to invisible in Kivronian society, they'd all be easy prey. Did Rafe have the right to shackle his brothers with loss and degradation? Position said yes, but he refused that tack. He growled and straightened the knot of white fabric at his throat.

Some strategy had to work. Rafe, now fully dressed, left his room and headed outside to clear his mind. One did not scorn the Council. Disobedience was unthinkable, yet he thought it.

Was insanity stripping away his logic? *Not yet. I won't destroy my brothers.*

There must be another option. If he agreed to release Pepper and bound the Kivronian female, he'd die inside and a new betrothal period would begin. *Ah, that could be Garmood's plan.* Another month or more before Rafe might be healed, but there was no time. Not for him. Each night brought another symptom. But how could Garmood know of the illness? The monster couldn't be sure, only suspect, unless someone talked.

He understood the persuasive skills of his enemy. The marring of Rafe's side was nothing to the scars on his soul. Few could withstand such piercing argument, most didn't try, but gave in.

Three people possessed information of Rafe's condition. His brothers would die before telling, and betrayal wasn't in Pepper. *And I'd know.* Garmood's reek didn't cling to her. No signs of physical damage to her or emotional turmoil warned him. Rafe couldn't read her thoughts, but his other senses remained. *Impossible. She wouldn't.* He'd know. Rafe shoved the idea from his mind. Garmood only guessed. It's that snake's strategy. There's no traitor.

Memories of that viper tormented him. If only Rafe could

remove Garmood. Tearing his heart out crossed Rafe's mind and a slow smile spread across his mouth. The creature's end would solve their problems, but confrontation at tonight's public ceremony was sure suicide. Garmood retained a cohort of fine warriors. They'd fell Rafe before he closed his fist around the fleshy organ. All Kivron would think him addled. If he survived the attempt, the Council would exterminate him for madness and treason.

He'd die a traitor expunged from the annals—like Hebric. Rafe's heart twisted.

"Silch." How to combat this? Rafe dragged his hand through his hair. He'd go to Kivron, appeal to the Council and offer the Lottery win to another male. If made to appear a great sacrifice, leadership may accept his passing on the new female. He'd have to humble himself and grovel. His jaw tightened. It would cost him respect. In his mental state, he couldn't think of another solution. He'd employ bribery, anything to sweeten his cause. But what could he offer the Council that they couldn't take?

Rafe found Dante securing the perimeter near the rock wall behind the woods. After finding the murdered woman, security had taken priority. He rehearsed the situation and awaited his brother's response.

"I see," said Dante. "How will you inform Pepper the trip's off, you're leaving, and she may be a free woman?"

"She won't be a free woman. I'll take care of that. Nothing will change."

"Are you sure of your decision? Releasing Pepper would solve our vulnerability and the advantages...."

"Stop," Rafe interrupted, irritation growing. "There are no advantages." Not to him.

Dante's face remained unreadable. "Have you considered everything?"

"I've made my decision."

"But is your logic intact?"

Rafe's control waned and anger flared. "Enough." A low growl rumbled in his chest. He leashed his frustration, ignored the voices, the whispers crying for violence. "I vowed to Pepper. We're bound and nothing will dissuade me. Don't test me, brother. My logic remains sharp. The Lottery has Garmood's thick fingers all over it. I feel the snare around my neck and refuse to be taken so easily. I'll fight to keep her."

Rafe breathed in the cool evening air and squelched insanity's call. "I'll leave for Kivron after Pepper and her sire reunite. That should lessen the blow of postponing our trip. I'll return with no harm done." He'd do whatever it took to insure that fact. Dante continued to stare at him without comment. Rafe narrowed his gaze. "Rather than giving me advice, shouldn't you be leaving to retrieve Dr. Morgan?"

"Directly. Do you have other orders?"

"Don't let him out of your sight."

Dante turned to go, then stopped and faced him. "I would never have believed it, but it's true, you're like the valiant *dragoste.* You're willing to sacrifice everything for her. You must love her very much."

Never had Rafe admitted tender feelings for a woman, but until Pepper, he'd never experienced any. Dante's perception unnerved him. "Am I that transparent?"

"To those who know you, yes."

"And those who don't, would they detect my feelings?"

"Your scent gives you away even if your words don't. "Dante sniffed. "You ooze the honeyed smell of love."

"How far away can you detect it?"

"Most Kivronians would pick it up in a large room, but especially any acquainted with your scent."

Vulnerability. Garmood laid in wait to entrap him. Blatant feelings for Pepper brought attention and put them both in jeopardy. She might be safer with him gone, unless…. "One more thing, protect Pepper. Garmood may have forced me to leave to get at her, but there's no choice. I'm commanded to go."

Dante bowed his head. "Done."

# # #

Pepper struggled with the zipper of the new, green dress. "Finally," she huffed, smoothing the fabric over her hips. Rafe thought it accentuated the emerald in her eyes. The cut did flatter her trim waist and the square neck hinted at cleavage without allowing exposure. The dress made her feel pretty. Or, did Rafe do that?

Even when she dressed in slouchy sweats, he often gazed at her with enough heat to singe her clothes. She straightened the hem above her knee. He told her often how beautiful she was and she believed him. It helped that his thoughts echoed his words. Rafe was an honest and good man, no reason to doubt his sincerity or love. She knew his heart.

She lifted her billow of auburn hair. Twisting the mass, she held it in place and forced a gold clip shut. "There." Not a Kivronian knot, but it kept threads from falling into her eyes.

What surprise did Rafe have for her? He'd slammed his mind shut and had focused on Garmood. She knew it for what it was, a distraction, but she still picked up a feeling. It was something big.

Were they flying in a private jet or did he have another extravagant gift? Intuition told her *bigger*. She tucked a wayward strand behind her ear. Something niggled, a feeling of upheaval. That could mean anything. Rafe's mind swirled in chaos brought on by either illness or by Garmood. Neither felt right. Her instincts argued between trouble and joy. How could it be both? Maybe excitement confused her intuition.

Pepper slipped into matching pumps and headed downstairs. Rafe would be waiting, impeccably dressed and outwardly in control. She'd finally meet the elusive Bram. They'd attend the Pledge of Loyalty and then she and Rafe would begin their travels. Excitement fluttered in her stomach. The trip didn't cause the butterflies, it was the thought of being alone with Rafe for the next two weeks, ending the betrothal. *Then, the real honeymoon.* Heat crept up her neck and into her face. *Stop it. You're acting like a schoolgirl.* She'd been with a man before—one.

A few moments later Pepper stared in disbelief and

blinked. What was *he* doing here? In the foyer stood Rafe with that arrogant, swaggering warrior she'd seen outside Garmood's office. This time the bad boy didn't undress her with his eyes, but kept himself in check. Good thing. Rafe would kill him for looking at her that way.

Rafe greeted her with a smile and took her hand. "Pepper, I'd like you to meet my brother, Bram."

Her eyes darted to Brams's face. So much like Rafe, yet nothing like him. How could she have missed the resemblance? Tall, dark-haired with the same Nucretah good looks and Kivronian perfection of all vampires. His bad-boy attitude exuded about his muscular frame, but no thoughts. None. Rafe must have warned him about her gift.

Bram narrowed his eyes and bowed his head to her. "My pleasure."

He recognized her, all right. His careful stance and guarded thoughts didn't hide the speculation in his eyes or the recognition. *Be nice, Pepper. He's family.* She pasted on a smile. "I've heard so much about you. I feel as if we've met."

Bram's eyes flashed.

"Not likely," said Rafe. "Bram's been away and will soon be off again."

She tried to read Rafe, but not so much as a trickle of insight emerged, and then Bram, but her probing met with steel walls. "I'm sorry I won't get the chance to know you."

"Yes," said Bram. "Unfortunate."

"You echo my thoughts," said Rafe, and drew his arm around her. "Darling, are you ready to go?"

Alarms rang in her head. Something was up. She needed a moment alone to make sense of her intuition. "In a minute, I just need to run upstairs and get my purse."

Pepper had reached the top of the stairs when thoughts pummeled her brain. Two distinct signatures, one Rafe's familiar pattern, the other Bram's. She stopped in the hall before her room and opened herself to their minds. It amazed her how simple mental eavesdropping had become, hearing them as clearly as regular conversation.

"You were right to warn us," said Bram. "Don't trust her. I saw her waiting outside Garmood's office the day I returned."

"Are you certain it was her?"

"Positive."

"How can you be sure? I've never known you to recall a human female."

"Pepper's different. I couldn't read her mind. I didn't know about her black hole status at the time. I thought... I thought it had to be something else."

Anger, resentment, and distrust assaulted her head and body from both men. *Traitor.*

Her stomach knotted as ugly thoughts sunk deep into her brain like the *Titanic,* pulled beneath virulent waves. Trembling, she opened the bedroom door and slipped inside.

Damn. Damn. Damn.

CHAPTER TWELVE

He trusted Bram above anyone, but this….Rafe closed his eyes and wrapped his fingers over the newel post in the foyer, waiting. *Not Pepper*. Disjointed thoughts spurred emotion mingled with madness. Had she lied to him all this time? Was he a besotted fool or had insanity ruined his basic instincts so that deceit had swept past, unseen?

He opened his eyes and fixed his gaze on the sculpture adjacent to the stairs, spires of black obsidian broken in half, the severed peaks littered the base of a crimson bowl. Is that what love did? Break a man, leaving him useless and bleeding?

Thank the deities, Bram had left. Rafe couldn't face him. Not with his chest torn open and his heart thudding in agony. Rafe never could hide anything from him. How he wished he possessed Dante's ability to mask his feelings expertly. He could use such skill tonight as he sat amongst the Kivronian elite, pretending his life hadn't ended.

What had he missed? Pepper had made a business arrangement, binding herself to him in exchange for her sire, nothing more. She held no allegiance to him. Had his arrogance convinced him otherwise? He shook his head in an effort to clear insanity's fog. Where was the truth? With his own skills tainted, Rafe had to rely on Bram's superior view. What a cruel turn of fate. The great warrior of Kivron, beaten by a human female.

No matter. Though she might despise him, he'd keep his end of the agreement and return her sire to her. And he'd honor the Council's ruling and accept the Lottery win. Pepper would be free of him. His brothers would be lifted in status, while he'd exist in a loveless union.

Unless insanity forced his extermination. *I can endure anything for the time remaining.*

A door upstairs closed and Rafe turned to gaze on the object of his destruction. Pepper's eyes were red. Had she cried? No doubt she'd heard Bram's accusation and gleaned Rafe's thoughts. She pitied him. *Always pity, never love.*

Her mouth tightened into a phony smile as she descended the stairs. He could grill her and force a confession. Why waste time and energy? He offered her his arm. "You heard."

She stared at him, chin trembling. "I'm sorry. I didn't..."

"Stop." What control he had, Rafe summoned to guard his mind and hurt. "Under the circumstances, our trip is cancelled.

You'll be relieved to know our binding is void. I've been called to Kivron and will leave before dawn."

Her eyes glistened. "But I thought binding was eternal."

How could she continue the farce? Did she enjoy twisting the knife in his heart to see him squirm? "Enough talk. There's no need. We both know the truth and after tonight you'll be rid of me."

She swiped at her eyes and opened her mouth to speak. Rafe couldn't bear to see her tears, even if they were a manipulation. "No more lies," he interrupted. "Let's go. We dare not be late and disrespect Garmood."

#

Surrounded by alien vampires, Pepper felt more alone at this moment than ever in her life. She trailed Rafe into the arena, formerly used for football and soccer, now the preferred stage for Kivronian games and large ceremonies. Tears blurred her vision. Throngs of people diffused into watery figures. Nothing was sharp, but Rafe's rejection, an ice pick stabbing between her ribs, macerating her heart. She wanted to curl up and die.

She didn't have the freedom to sob until her tears were spent. No. Rafe required her silent presence to keep Garmood at bay. Maybe she owed Rafe that. What a mess she'd made of things. All because she refused to be patient and just get to know him, listening instead to her fear. She'd justified meeting Garmood and had shunned trust. Her father had warned her that rejecting love would hurt in the end. As always, he'd been spot-on. She wished he were here.

They took their seats in a private box overlooking the field. Rows of warriors, clad in white uniforms, filled the benches below. Bram was among them. She couldn't blame Bram for trying to protect Rafe, but damned if she would keep quiet and allow Rafe to cast her off because of a misunderstanding. She hadn't betrayed him.

Trumpets blared. Warriors stood, each carrying their family's banner. Colors of green, gold, red, violet and blue wafted in the evening breeze, the smell of rain in the air. Overhead lights cast shadows while illuminating the action. She couldn't appreciate the pageantry. "Rafe."

He didn't respond, but fixated on the masses below.

"If you don't allow me to answer these allegations, I'll… I'll." What could she do? "I'll make a scene."

Nothing. He'd clamped his mind shut.

What now? He'd called her bluff. "Hear me out. You're

known to be a fair man. Even on Earth we give the accused the right to defend himself."

That got his attention. He turned and considered her. "Very well. After the ceremony."

Intuition warned that if she didn't speak here, she'd never get the chance. "Now."

He raised a single brow. "Speak."

"I admit to trying to meet with Garmood, but I changed my mind. I haven't spoken to him."

"You changed your mind? Why?"

"I'd waited for hours. I wondered about the wisdom of interviewing Garmood for information when Bram went right in ahead of me. It made me angry and I left." She touched his arm. "That's all there is to it."

"I warned you to avoid him." He cleared his throat. "We were bound and yet you sought him out. Why should I believe you?"

"Because it's the truth."

"Truth?" His eyes flashed. "I doubt you understand the concept."

Rafe's comment stung. She released her grip on his arm. Misty rain fell, dampening everything, but her resolve. The crowd erupted in hisses. Garmood, dressed in black robes, his red hair hanging over his shoulders, strutted through the group of warriors, and claimed the center seat in his box at the far end of the field.

This wasn't going well, but Pepper refused to give up. "What can I do to convince you?"

Rafe didn't look at her. "Proof."

"How can I prove I didn't see him?"

He shrugged. "That's what I require."

The oversized dignitary raised his hand to silence the crowd. "As my special guest, I've invited a great man, a Kivronian by heart, if not by birth. Show respect for Dr. Daniel Morgan."

"No." Rafe growled and leaned forward, his body as tight as a drawn bow.

Pepper craned her neck to see. Her father appeared beside Garmood wearing his white lab coat. *The color for loyalty.* "It's true. He's here!"

Rafe glared at her. "This was your price for betraying me?"

"No. I would never. I'm as shocked as you are."

Garmood roared and silence fell over the throng. "I invite his daughter, Pepper, to join us on the stand."

Devastation haunted Rafe's features. "I almost believed you." Waves of agony and betrayal poured from him. "Garmood's waiting." He looked away. "Leave me."

Tears spilled over her cheeks and she fled from the box toward the field.

# # #

The sea of warriors parted as Rafe watched his heart run to the arms of her sire. Though his lungs compressed and his head pounded with prodding to jump the rail and throttle Garmood. Rafe stayed put. No one would learn anything from his reaction. Stone-faced, he shackled the voices in his brain. If Pepper had told the truth, Rafe couldn't tell.

Perhaps madness had made inroads to his senses. Sense would be the last to go before.... But Garmood had called her to his side and she ran to him. That laid guilt on her. But what if this too was part of Garmood's plan? Rafe shoved through mania's hold on his mind to grasp sanity.

That viper. If he shanghaied Dr. Morgan, then what had become of Dante?

A shiver of ice ran up his spine. Sweat beaded his brow, trickled down his neck, and beneath his collar. Oath after oath escaped his clenched teeth. Rafe strode from his box, shoving in desperation past bodies to save his younger brother. *My fault.* He should have suspected and sent an armed regiment to retrieve Pepper's sire. What had he been thinking? *The insufferable madness.* At every turn it thwarted his efforts. And now Garmood had in his hands the means to know Rafe's every weakness, including information regarding the insurgents and Talon's identity. Garmood would wring the truth from her lips in short order. And what of Dante?

Rafe knew his enemy. Dante was young and capable, but not against the likes of Garmood. Even at Rafe's best, he'd be lucky to survive battling that monster. And he was far from his best. Nothing to be done about that. He escaped from the arena and barreled down a darkened hall. Grabbing his communicator in shaky hands, he prayed to the Kivronian deities and called Dante. When the device showed unavailable, he called the transport station.

"Commander Dante never arrived," said the voice.

Rafe threw his fist into the wall. Fragments of the communicator propelled in all directions. "Useless technology." He needed Bram. But his brother waited to pledge loyalty to the snake. Yanking Bram out of the ceremony would land them both in prison. Just what Garmood wanted, all three

Nuctretah's in his power.

Insanity screamed between Rafe's ears. Hunger gnawed. His claws lengthened and fangs erupted, prepared for slaughter. Strength and the promise of invincibility seduced him. *Give in. Destroy your enemies—all of them.* He covered his ears to deny the murderous voices in his head and leaned against the wall. "No," he breathed. "I'm in control."

Fighting mania, he sunk to the ground, inches away from succumbing. Visions played behind his eyes, Hebric grasping his severed leg, Garmood slicing into Rafe's side to drag out his guts, and the sight of his sisters' slayings. Burning seethed his bones. He needed an anchor, something to stop his plunge into oblivion.

Pepper.

After everything, he still loved her. Had she lied or had Garmood seized an opportunity and made things appear that way? He pulled his mind from destruction and dwelled on the sweet memories of Pepper's laughter as she learned to shoot, of hearing the playful tone in her voice as she teased him, or remembering her passion-drugged eyes after his kiss. Pepper, his lifeline to reality, pulled him from the dark precipice into light.

Physically weak and damp with rain and sweat from the ordeal, Rafe struggled to his feet. Time was short, but if Dante were alive, he'd find him.

Rafe stalked the transporter station and the soaked parking lot. The scent of wet asphalt mingled with Kivronian males and humans. Another piece of rotten luck, the shower threatened to destroy evidence and there was already precious little of it. Garmood's men had been careful. Rafe let a burst of oaths fly into the night. He didn't care who heard. He might have days or only moments before madness overtook him. He had to find Dante and free him from the evil clutches of Garmood before the monster had time to abuse him. Rafe knew what horrors awaited his brother.

Memories and the rain pummeled him. Cold water, sopping his uniform couldn't compete with the freeze, which already numbed his flesh. He'd seen enough a century ago in the dank cavern where Garmood had held him for months. Brave men sustained flaying of skin, and severed limbs, but few survived when their organs were dragged from their bodies for Garmood's twisted enjoyment. Rafe had endured that agony.

Only with help from the deities had Bram rescued Rafe

before death took him. *What good had it done?* Rafe's heart convulsed. He'd held his tongue, kept his sisters' hiding place secret, but to no avail. While Bram rescued him, Garmood raped and murdered the women of his family. His life had come at too high a price. Had the monster's murderous acts occurred after civil war decimated the female population, Garmood would've been executed and expunged.

Rafe closed his eyes to resend the vision and let his senses open. *Blood, faint but definite.* He spied a few watered down drops on the blacktop and reached down to dip in his finger. He sniffed. *Dante's.* His brother knew what Garmood planned for him. Rafe shuddered. The same as he planned for all of them, given the opportunity.

With Dante captured and little time for rescue, every moment became an eternity. Rafe's claws lengthened, the overhead lights glinted off their sharp edges in the rain. Insane voices drifted in and out of his mind calling for death. And Rafe longed to comply. But he harnessed his strength and crushed the whispers like sand beneath his boot. *Silence--for now.*

Where had they taken Dante? The factory, Garmood's estate or a myriad of other locations in Red Rock? There was no way to know. Rafe shook his head, flinging water from his hair. He needed Bram's tracking skills, but even Bram needed a scent. Blood was best, but would this drop be enough? Bram had tracked Rafe and he'd find Dante. They would rescue him. No acceptable alternative existed.

Rafe returned to the arena and strode to the entrance, struggling with each step to conquer the urge for violence. *Stay alert, save Dante and then destroy the enemy.* Rafe's extermination didn't matter, not if he killed Garmood.

# # #

Pepper embraced her father, hoping for comfort, but found worry. He'd grown thin, his hazel eyes shadowed with fear as his thoughts flowed into her, threats made against her life to guarantee his cooperation. She lifted her head from his shoulder, damp with rain and her tears. He dabbed her face with the hem of his lab coat. "There, there," he croaked. "It's all right. Everything will be all right."

"Oh, father, you're home." Streams ran freely from her eyes and down her face. "How long?" she choked through sobs. Feeling his arms around her was everything she'd hoped it would be, filled with the comforting love she'd needed.

He hesitated and glanced at Garmood before answering.

"For a while."

Her skin prickled at the back of her neck. She blinked past the moisture blurring her vision and gazed at her father's face. *What was her father hiding*? The question carried with it the answer. Rafe, not Garmood had planned her father's visit. *Kidnapping. Capture. Dante.* Her blood chilled as the situation formed in her mind.

Oh, no.

Rafe's memories of torture played back in her head. Her stomach plummeted like a stone tossed down a ravine. She resisted the urge to vomit. No matter what disgusting game Garmood played, she couldn't act at odds with her father's return. She forced a smile. Garmood didn't know she read thoughts. Best to guard her gift. Surprise and intuition might lead her to Dante and free them all. It was their best shot.

Meaty fingers clasped her shoulder. Her stomach rolled and she wanted to jerk away. *Breathe. Relax.* Her father was home. She was ecstatic for his return, but Garmood had spoiled the reunion. Pepper had to pull herself together and act happy.

"My dear, you're shaken," said Garmood. "I hope my surprise hasn't overcome you."

Pepper slapped on her best fake smile. "I'm all right. I just didn't expect this." *Be happy. Be happy, damn it.*

"Of course." The behemoth leveled his yellow, tiger's eyes on her and pointed to a seat beside him. "You'll have plenty of time with you sire after the ceremony." *Ungrateful female.*

She almost sighed with relief when she heard Garmood's thoughts, proof her gift might be good for something. She stretched her smile. "Thank you. I'm still in shock. I can't tell you how I appreciate all you've done." She didn't dare say what she really thought. *Monster.*

Moment by moment, Pepper excavated in Garmood's slimy mind and unearthed facts. Dante had been taken to the dignitary's estate awaiting skillful extraction of information. Thunder rumbled, lightening flashed, and storm clouds burst. The ceremony wasn't called on account of rain. She sat beside Garmood, getting soaked, and willed her mind to wade into the creature's thoughts, a spatter here, a drizzle there until she learned the exact location of Dante's prison in a remote corner of the basement of his estate.

Her wet hair fell from the weight, the gold clip stuck somewhere in the dripping strands. She bit her lip in concentration. She'd wanted to join the fight for freedom and had gotten her wish. Dante's life may depend on her. But how to relay the message?

Bram glared at her as he approached to pledge loyalty with a string of warriors. He might be her only chance. Garmood intended to keep her close. He intended a good many things, all of which turned her stomach. *What to do?* Passing Bram a note was impossible and too obvious. It might get them killed. She fisted her hands in her lap. *Think.* Sweat ran down her sides. A scene. *That's it.* She'd create a scene to distract Garmood.

Bram knelt before them with his hand to his throat in a pledge. What ever she was going to do, she had to do it now.

Pepper leapt onto Bram, propelling them both back and onto the field. Bram stared back at her in amazement and then hardened his gaze. "What are you up to?"

She lay sprawled on top of him in the mud. Thunder rumbled. "Captured," she breathed, all but silent against his ear. "Dante. Garmood's estate." She hoped Bram heard and no one else. Thunder had combined with the crowd's laughter when she'd flung herself on him.

With the shock worn off, warriors surrounded them. "Liar," she yelled, reared up and slapped Bram hard. "You two-timing, arrogant dog. How could you? You broke my heart." She pounded his chest with her fists. Rain coursed down her face, her hands stung from beating on him. She had to convince Garmood.

Burly aliens pulled her off Bram and deposited her back on her chair. Garmood appeared amused, his amber eyes full of speculation, his mind entertaining lascivious thoughts. Bram stood, his formerly pristine uniform, caked with mud. He smirked like a bad boy caught throwing rocks at a neighbor's cat, arrogant and unapologetic.

With bushy red brows lowered, Garmood stared at Bram and drummed his fingers on the arm of his chair. "Nucretah, have you made advances to your brother's mate?"

"I didn't know she was his mate at the time." Bram shrugged and gave her a flirtatious wink.

The onlookers snickered. They enjoyed Bram's antics and it helped sell her outrage. "Liar," she shrieked, stomped her foot and then turned her attention on Garmood. "Please, make him leave. I can't stand the sight of him."

From beneath the protective awning of his seat, Garmood wheezed. "Agreed. He's distracting from the event. But if Rafe desires satisfaction, I require a battle for all to witness. And Bram, in the future, you might choose your indiscretions more carefully."

"Lord Garmood." Bram bowed, retrieved the soggy Nucretah banner, and swaggered from the field.

Murmurs bounced from the walls of the stadium along with Kivronian thoughts. Pepper swayed on her seat from the weight of conjecture and sexual innuendo. Rafe had the right to slit Bram's throat for what she'd accused him of. It was a huge risk, but she had to pass the information to Bram and have him expelled from the arena. From Bram's thoughts, she knew he'd gotten the message.

Pepper sank back in the damp, red velvet chair and realized Garmood stared at her, wondering what had transpired between her and Bram. Her charade continued. Leaning toward him, she wiped dirt from her cheek with her wet fingers and smiled. "Thank you for your help. You're kind to consider my feelings and position."

Garmood leered, training his gaze on her soaked chest as another line of warriors approached. "My dear, your position has never left my mind since we met at the binding."

"Oh," she mumbled, and noticed what Garmood found so interesting. She was cold and her nipples pushed into the wet fabric, making the dress appear all too much like green skin.

She stared ahead wrapping her arms over her embarrassment.

He chuckled, the rusty sound of hinges grating her nerves. Garmood's thoughts oozed over her like filthy grease. Her stomach churned. He watched the warriors pledge loyalty as he placed his meaty palm on her bare knee. Tremors raced through her body. Intuition clanged alarms in her head. The beast had plans for her, ugly, disgusting plans.

CHAPTER THIRTEEN

"Are you sure that's everything? Did Pepper say where on Garmood's estate?" Rafe pressed Bram as they sped down the highway in the Bentley, the tires spewing water in their wake.

"That's everything, except for public assault and accusing me of gross impropriety."

"You must admit her tactics worked."

"Yes." Bram scowled and zipped up the front of his black battle suit in favor of the too-visible dress white. "You're ordered to take your humiliation out of my hide in the arena."

"After I take Garmood's head."

"It's strange." Bram checked his weapons. "Why would she seek out Garmood only to betray him?"

Rafe had mulled over what occurred on the field. "Not strange, simple. She told the truth. Pepper never met with Garmood and she's out to prove her loyalty by helping save Dante."

"Or trap us."

Rafe spared him a glance. "Did you smell a lie on her?"

"No."

"Then we can trust her."

"Do we have a choice?" Bram slid weapons into his belt.

"Not if we want to save our brother," said Rafe.

"You couldn't sense the truth when you confronted her?" said Bram.

Rafe focused on the road. "I...wasn't sure."

"You doubted your ability."

Rafe breathed out and shifted gears to take a steep climb. "Insanity fogs my mind, thwarts my senses and strength. I doubt myself, but not Pepper, not now."

Bram checked his Nova sword's charge. "I like her."

"Really?"

"She's inventive. Much like myself."

"And Garmood has her." Every muscle in Rafe's body tensed. "I won't leave without Pepper."

Bram nodded. "And Dr. Morgan?"

"He's in no real danger. The High Council values the work he's doing. Dr. Morgan is close to solving our human breeding problem."

"Amazing. You and Pepper might have young?"

"If we survive."

"How is it that you're not cured?" Bram studied him like

signs on a difficult trail. "I'm sure she loves you. I feel it."

"I'm hanging by a thread." The conversation taunted vile murmurs in his head, but he gagged them to silence. He still had control. "Pepper hasn't admitted her love, even to herself."

"And you suffer."

"Not for long."

"No." Bram glared at him. "It won't come to that."

Rafe ignored his brother's denial. "After Dante and Pepper are free...." Rafe struggled, the words sticking in his throat. "Remember your promise."

They pulled off the road and concealed the car among pines and oak. Rafe's damp uniform stuck to his skin. The rain had stopped. Wind stripped water from branches and pelted them as they maneuvered through the foliage. The turrets of the estate loomed ahead. Dante lay imprisoned behind the red stone walls.

All they had to do was scale the battlements, subdue the guards, and find their brother without being detected. And then escape. Their chances were slim. Rafe's were less than that. He pushed ahead of Bram, taking the lead and putting space between them. If insanity flared and Rafe were reduced to a rabid beast, better that Bram had time to notice and to protect himself.

# # #

The fortress was chilly, dark and had the feel of a medieval castle. Vampires built it to house visiting Kivronian officials. Humans did the backbreaking work and the lives lost in construction were tallied as unfortunate accidents to the alien, food supply. Pepper shivered from the memory as much as from the cold. The blood tax had been high that year.

Was this their prison? No matter how beautiful the surroundings, no one left without Garmood's permission. The rock walls of the fortress pressed upon her mind as Pepper and her father bid each other good night. Garmood denied them a moment's privacy. How like the alien occupiers to deny a tender moment between father and daughter. Goosebumps dotted her skin. Her green dress dripped water onto the floor. Thud. Thud. Thud. Each drop mimicking the sound of her heart, rhythmic, fast.

Her father looked miserable. His white lab coat hung over his arm leaking water onto the marble floor. His worn, brown suit was rumpled and damp. There was much to say, but no chance to say anything. He wrapped his arms around her and hugged her tight. "I'll see you in the morning."

His thoughts encased her in warmth and love. How she'd missed him. Pepper embraced him, wishing time would stop and she could extend this moment forever. "Bright and early for breakfast." She gazed into his hazel eyes and smiled, trying to appear brave.

"No one can make eggs and toast like you do, honey." His mouth trembled and then twisted into a pitiful smile.

"Dr. Morgan," Garmood grunted, their signal to part company. "It's time you took your rest. This is a working trip, not vacation."

Her father's shoulders slumped in defeat. "Very well."

Pepper watched him climb the stairs and disappear out of view. She'd be lucky to visit with her father at all. The Council required him to put in twelve-hour days. His lab, complete with assistants, was set up on the premises. She didn't have a head for science, but she understood that her father's work would change everything between humans and vampires.

She rubbed her temples with the pads of her fingers. Her head ached from Garmood's repulsive thoughts. Rest sounded good, but she couldn't afford to let down her guard. Dante was chained to a wall downstairs and she had to find him. "I'm tired." She accentuated a yawn. Pepper tilted her head and tried to appear innocent. She'd picked through Garmood's brain and knew he had no intention of letting her leave, but couldn't let on. If he knew she could read his mind, he'd slit her throat.

In three strides he closed the space between them and towered over her like a redwood tree. "You'll stay."

She refused to be intimidated, or at least refused to show it. She lifted her chin and stood taller. "Rafe will worry." Doubtful, considering their last conversation, but Garmood didn't know that.

"I've sent word. He knows you're with me."

Liar.

If Bram had received her message and had told Rafe, they might believe she'd told the truth, if not, she and Dante would have a long stay in prison. She ran her hands over her chilled arms. "Well, it would be easier to see my father if I stayed."

"It's settled. There's a room already prepared. Allow me to show you."

Intuition shouted warnings. How could she avoid him? "I usually read before bed. Is there a library here?"

"No. We don't think much of Earth literature." He slid his thick palm against her torso and smiled. "But I might find something for you."

That's what she feared. His mind pulsed with sexual conquest as he spirited her down a darkened hall. "Your room is adjacent to mine."

Of course it was. How could she find Dante and free him with the red-haired ogre next door? Garmood flung open a door with his free hand and maneuvered her inside. The lock clicked and her heart raced. A bed filled the small room. No other decoration touched the room, but a tiny window cut out of stone with black bars that marred the view. A lone wooden chair hugged the wall beside the door. Garmood recklessly shoved her and she stumbled on her heels. "Sit before you fall down."

Pepper collapsed on the chair, her legs quaking.

Garmood's congenial smile vanished, replaced by the look of a man intent on no good. His eyes narrowed. Not in the impersonal way of a stalking tiger, but in the ruthless manner of a man seeking revenge. *I'll make Rafe suffer.* The words stuck in her head like oily sludge.

He leaned over her, and strategically placed his large hands on either side of the chair caging her in, and bared huge canines. An obvious threat. She shied away, but he grabbed her hair in one hand and yanked back, exposing her throat. *I could take her blood*. The thought filled her mind like red haze. Instinct forced her to struggle, but he tightened his fist in her hair and ran his tongue along the outer ridge of her ear. "I have a proposition for you."

Her pulse roared in her ears. She was in no position to refuse. Pepper wanted to close her eyes to shut him out, but didn't dare. Any moment, he might pierce her neck with his fangs. Hot breath dampened her skin as he rubbed his teeth lightly over her throat. She gasped, but couldn't utter a word.

He licked down the side of her neck to the crease of her shoulder. "What's Rafe's life worth to you?"

Her stomach knotted. She refused to look at him, but Garmood grabbed her face in his hand, and twisted her head to meet his gaze. The strength in his fingers warned he could crush her skull if he chose. "Why?" she mumbled, against his hand. He relaxed the grip on her face, but still held her.

"I ask the questions here, not you." His fingers squeezed. Pressure built until she feared her jaw would splinter.

She moaned, and he released his hold on her face and hair, leaving her to massage her sore flesh. His mouth twisted into an ugly smirk. "I'm sure you feel something for Rafe and that poses an interesting dilemma for you."

"What are you talking about?" Garmood's thoughts seeped into her mind, but nothing decipherable beyond raw hate.

The smirk grew into a sly smile. "My men captured Rafe outside before we arrived, unfortunately Bram escaped, but two Nucretahs will do."

Pepper's heart slammed against her ribs. Rafe in Garmood's claws, nothing could be worse. "You're going to kill them."

Garmood raised his rust-colored brows. "What else? Unless you accept my offer."

Her intuition screamed. Her gut twisted and her body begged her to run. She trembled on the chair. "What do you want?" The knot in her stomach grew to a ball of ice.

"Publicly denounce Rafe as your mate and choose me." His tongue slid over his lips. "And then I let them live."

Pepper felt sick. Words flew into her brain. *Revenge. Torture.* The ice in her stomach rolled freezing her insides. "Rafe will never agree."

"He has no say in the matter. Until the betrothal is over, it's your choice." Garmood extended his vicious claws. They lengthened before her eyes to a wicked four inches. "Refuse him publicly, and say you prefer me."

Bile rose in her throat and she forced it down. "Not even in your dreams."

"Don't try me." Clutching her upper arms, he dragged her from the chair. She wobbled on her toes. "I can make your existence pleasure or pain." He held her tight with his thick fingers, bruising her skin. His lethal glare nearly enough to immobilize her.

Tears pooled in her eyes. What could she do? This vampire didn't make idle threats. "Don't force me to do this."

"I'll make this easy for you. Refuse me and Dante dies." Evil stared at her from his yellow gaze. "Ah, but not Rafe, not right away. I think I'll torture him for a while, yes, mutilate him."

"You wouldn't."

"My dear, I'd enjoy it. I could kill him, of course, but if I slice his pretty face, gouge out an eye, and leave him to scar in the sun, yes."

Tears clogged her throat. "You're a monster."

"True enough," he sneered. "How will you feel knowing Rafe suffered and you had the power to save him, but chose against it? I almost hope you refuse me. Maiming Nucretah will take many nights and you'll be by my side and watch."

"No." Her lips moved, but terror silenced her.

"Accept my offer and they live. You have an hour." Garmood set her on her feet, flashed his canines in warning, and left.

Pepper trembled. Her mind a mass of panicked confusion. What could she do? *Calm down and think.* Adrenaline surged through her like a roller coaster, all steep climbs and sharp turns, until she felt upside down with her stomach in her throat. *I will not throw up.* She pressed her fist to her gut. *Think.*

There was no choice, not really. If she didn't agree to Garmood's demands, Dante would die and Rafe might wish he had. Garmood's graphic description sickened her. Eternity bound to that beast was the price to save them. She shuddered. This was a nightmare.

CHAPTER FOURTEEN

Blinding pain stabbed behind Rafe's eyes. He squinted in the dim light and forced his burning orbs to register his surroundings. *Silch.* The dungeon of the fortress, complete with torture devices and a dank, moldy smell he recalled from when he'd inspected last year.

Heavy chains covered with silver bit into his wrists and ankles, eating away at his skin. He lifted his head. It throbbed and his stomach lurched. *Movement, a bad idea.* He closed his eyes and lowered his head to the cold concrete slab. The last Rafe remembered, he'd been standing outside planning his ascent over the wall. One of Garmood's men must have hit him from behind.

Where was Bram? Rafe peeled open his lids and surveyed the room. He was alone, but someone had been there. Manacles hung from the wall and a pool of blood congealed beneath. Heart pounding, Rafe breathed in the scent. *Dante.*

Rafe arched his back, swore through clenched teeth, and yanked hard against his shackles, straining with all his might, but to no avail. Was Dante dead or had Garmood only moved him? The amount of fluid on the ground argued against survival. Rafe refused to believe it. Dante lived. He must. Now, if Rafe could do the same.

Foggy-headed, Rafe waded past the pounding in his skull to recall fragments of memory. How did he get here? Bram had escaped. Help would be coming. If any man had skill and resources to free them, it would be Bram, but time ran short. Garmood would be ruthless when he returned.

The monster took particular delight in torturing Rafe. He was the image of his sire, and that accident of birth enraged Garmood. If the viper couldn't kill Cadder, he'd wipe out his sons as he'd murdered the Nucretah women a century ago. *All over my mother.*

Any woman with sense would choose Cadder over Garmood. And Rafe's mother had had sense. No betrothal laws had been broken, nothing amiss there, yet Garmood refused to move on. He fed his hurt on Nucretah blood. In a way, Rafe could understand the anger of loosing a mate to an enemy. But not the violence of killing her.

Garmood wouldn't have gotten away with his butchery, except that Rafe's sire had been arrogant and foolish as a young man. Cadder had bested a warrior in battle, belittled and humbled him before thousands. Who could have guessed that the warrior would live to rule as President of Kivron? And as Garmood extracted his revenge, the President turned a blind eye.

And what of Pepper? Rafe shuddered to think what she might be enduring at the moment. He'd seen what remained of his sisters and mother. Bile surged into his throat and he choked it down. How could any man, having loved a woman, turn that affection into hate and tear her apart with it? Garmood was capable of anything and it worried him.

Heavy footfalls alerted and Rafe turned his aching head to see his enemy. Garmood nudged Rafe's side with the toe of his boot. "You're awake. Where should we begin?"

Rafe scowled up at his opponent. "Where's Dante?"

"Not your concern, but I will tell you that he's still alive, not that he's enjoying the experience." Garmood grinned, an evil expression that darkened his features and his soulless, yellow eyes. He'd covered his clothes with the rust-brown gear worn at the processing plant to protect against stains. Not a surprise. There would be blood. "Let's begin with something slow and excruciating, but not lethal. That comes later." Garmood glanced to the darkening pool on the floor. "You,

Nucretah, have a high tolerance for pain."

"Crimwad." Rafe burned with anger and yanked at his chains to get at Garmood. The cuffs cut deep into his skin. It didn't matter, he could block the irritation, but worry for Dante and Pepper tortured him. Finally, his arms and legs fell back against the cold slab, exhausted. His breath, heavy from exertion.

"Finished?" Garmood stared under heavy, red brows. "You've grown weak. No wonder Pepper is refusing you."

"No," Rafe growled. He railed against his enemy's taunt and the insane voices pushing him to give in to the power of madness. *Break the chains and wrap them tight around Garmood's thick neck.* Rafe shackled the prodding and willed himself back to sanity. Was this Garmood's plan, to take Pepper from him? His heart wrenched. He couldn't allow it, no matter what the cost to him.

"You should've returned to Kivron by now and realized the Lottery win was a hoax." Garmood lengthened his claws. "Really Nucretah, have you lost your edge? Pepper will refuse you to your face and accept me as her mate. How fortunate that her father will make it possible for her to give me children." He flashed his claws in the overhead light. "Since you've made yourself available, I'll give Pepper incentive to agree, just as Cadder convinced my mate centuries ago. Shall we begin?"

# # #

It took less than five minutes to decide in favor of Garmood's heinous proposal, but Pepper hoped it wouldn't come to that. She shivered at the idea. In his arrogance, the beast had left the door unlocked, thinking a human female no threat to the likes of a powerful Kivronian warrior. "Insufferable, egocentric, red-haired ogre." She'd prove him wrong.

Pepper kicked off her soggy shoes and tiptoed into the hall, her bare feet as cold as the stone floor. She crept down the corridor, staying in the shadows and opened her mind in search of mental signals. Nothing close. Detecting none of Garmood's thoughts, she let her shoulders relax from their position up around her ears.

With every step, she hugged the rough rock walls until she came upon the backstairs and slinked down. Sweat moistened her hands, her face, and ran down her sides as she crept toward the basement. Being a black hole proved useful. None of the vampires had detected her. She searched for Dante from Garmood's map in her head. Once she found him, they'd recover Rafe and escape. Unfortunately, she had no idea how. *First things first.*

Dante should be in a small room down the corridor. Her gut twisted and she focused her intuition on what lay behind the metal door to her right. Something was very wrong.

Not Dante—Rafe.

No. No. No. She screamed in her head and shoved the door open, stumbling into the dark room. She blinked to adjust her vision. Rafe lay a few feet away on the ground. *Oh, no.* She ran to his side desperate to ease his discomfort. The tang of alien blood hung in the room, but he wasn't dead. Rafe's chaotic mind was working.

Pepper trembled at his suffering and closed herself off. The sight unnerved her enough. Burns and ragged cuts marred his bare torso. Sweat melded with blood, smearing his skin. How had he survived? Tears clouded her view and she tore her gaze from his brutalized body to his face. She had to pull herself together. "Rafe," she breathed. "Can you hear me?"

He opened his eyes, one blood-shot, and the other, too swollen to tell.

"Can you walk?"

Chains. The thought entered her mind.

Pepper frantically searched his arms and legs, and found cuffs, but nothing attached to them. "You're not chained." That might be good news, but her gut warned that Garmood would return soon. She had to hurry.

"Dante," he whispered.

"We'll find him. Can you walk? I don't think I can carry you."

Rafe contorted in pain and groaned when she helped him to his feet. Swaying, he leaned against her, his arm over her shoulder, her arm wrapped around his side. She'd never seen him so weak. Flashes of the torture he'd endured racked her mind and she almost lost her footing from the horror. Rafe slammed shut the door to his thoughts. That took energy and he had none to spare. She knew it.

With each step, Rafe clenched his jaw, but made no sound. He was beyond stoic. Her chest ached for his suffering. Only a foot away from the door, then down the corridor, through the double doors to the delivery bay and freedom, Rafe's thoughts confirmed the map in her head.

The hall seemed miles long. They'd been lucky so far, slipping through without detection. But for how long? Pepper scanned for mental chatter, and found her father three floors up, and someone in the delivery bay, maybe a guard. She swallowed fear. Where were Dante and Garmood?

Perspiration dotted Rafe's brow. He winced when they pushed through the double doors into the delivery area. Sparse lighting, shelves of boxes, and large wooden crates filled the space. Good for hiding. She bumped against his side. He flinched. *Broken ribs.* Pepper read his mind and nodded her apology. He forced a smile.

God, I love this man.

Her breath stilled and she stared into his anguished face. *I love him. I absolutely love this man and we may not make it out of here.* Her heart lodged in her throat. She should tell him, but every sound risked capture. Once they'd escaped, she'd admit her feelings. But what if…? *No.* She refused to think it. They'd get out. So close, so very close.

They concealed themselves behind crates of blood. The area appeared deserted, but her mind heard the musings of someone poring over paperwork. Rafe leaned against a crate and licked his lips. His hunger pelted her brain. Of course, he needed blood and they stood next to an ample supply, but they couldn't chance tearing into the crate, too much noise. They'd be caught.

Damn. Damn. Damn. Pepper couldn't believe what she was considering. She hated giving blood when it was only a vile full from her arm. She shuddered. *Just a little, enough to strengthen him.* Planting herself before Rafe, she pulled up her mass of hair and bared her neck.

He blinked as if confused. She dared not speak, but tilted her jaw and indicated her neck. He shook his head in denial, studied her face and let his gaze fall to her throat. She held firm and closed her eyes.

A sting to her neck followed by warmth spread from his bite and over her skin. Euphoria replaced fear in her mind as he took her blood. Rafe held her upright and she melted against him. "I love you." Had she said that out loud? Her mind joined with his. Blood flowed from her veins into his mouth. Her skin tingled. He drank and with each draw she felt strength flood into him. Her brain fogged. *So tired.* Would it be enough? Darkness shrouded her mind and took her into oblivion.

# # #

Rafe's energy returned with each swallow of her blood. His body needed to heal, but that required more than she could give. He'd stop before he put her in danger. *Drink. Take.* The voices in his head tempted. *More. Save yourself, and then kill Garmood.* Rafe gulped her offering. Rich flavor was addictive to his impoverished body. He needed, how he needed. Another sip and he'd let go. Then he could protect her. One more draw. *No. I love her.* He jerked his mouth away, the ruby flow beckoned to insanity. *Take it all.*

Her eyes were closed. Her breath was shallow and her skin, too pale. He relegated the whispers to a dark corner of his mind and licked the residue from her neck, sealing the flood. *Silch.* Madness and need had pushed him to take. He'd put her at risk. She wouldn't die. His feelings for her had halted his ravenous hunger and collared the madness just in time.

She slumped against him, her weight held in his arms. He'd have to carry her, avoid detection, escape, and find Bram. And somehow retrieve Dante. Rafe had been in tougher spots and they all had involved Garmood.

Rafe cradled Pepper's limp form against his chest. Sticky rust-red smears covered his body. He knew there would be blood, but he wished it had been Garmood's. Shrugging his shoulders, Rafe filled his lungs with air. *No pain.* His ribs were healed. How? Even fresh blood couldn't account for the speed of recovery. Gazing on Pepper in his arms, his heart clenched at her willingness to sacrifice for him. She'd know his need, had felt it. She understood his tenuous grasp on sanity, and yet had offered her life when madness could force him to drain her. The courage of this fragile beauty awed him. *If only—wait.* A vision drifted through his mind as if from a dream.

She loved him.

Was illness playing a foul trick or had he heard her confession during his frenzy to feed? Madness, fatigue, all the mental chaos burned away like fog evaporated by sunlight. He evicted doubt. Nothing but her love held such power. *Thank the deities.* Rafe dipped his head and pressed a kiss to her cheek. She'd rescued him from dreaded insanity, but could he save her?

Carrying Pepper in his arms, he crept toward the exit on his left. The eye scan would admit him and the door would open to freedom. Once he secured her safety, he'd go after Dante. Lining up with the device, Rafe waited, his heart pounded with anticipation and with a sense that danger stood near, lurking like a predator ready to pounce. His body was wary. The locks released. Rafe adjusted Pepper in his arms and grabbed the steel handle of the portal.

"Hold."

Rafe ignored the command and thrust open the exit. A clawed hand dug into the muscles of his shoulder.

"I said, 'hold'." Garmood added pressure. Blood dripped down Rafe's skin to the top of his slacks, still damp with sweat and his drying blood. He froze, refusing to endanger Pepper.

"Stealing from me, Nucretah?" Garmood leaned over Rafe's back. "Drop her."

"No." Rafe longed to rip the viper's hand from him, his arm too, but he'd wait. He needed time to regain full strength.

"Face me like a warrior." Garmood hit a switch on the wall and the escape hatch slammed and locked. "You're in no shape to fight me. I'll drag you both to the chamber, have you chained, and let you watch while I bind Pepper as my mate and claim her body."

Fury blazed to a red haze in Rafe's mind. Not madness, but the instinct to protect his mate. He turned to stare at the monster, now stripped of protective clothing, and changed to the formal uniform of a binding ritual. *Presumptuous snake.* Earlier, Rafe would've guaranteed Pepper's refusal of Garmood, but no longer. She'd sacrifice herself to this disgusting creature so Rafe might live. Her actions and his healing proved she loved him. Living didn't exist without her.

She was his heart. With Pepper in his enemy's bed, Rafe would rather suffer disgrace by being wiped from the annals than to take his next breath. "No." Rafe bared his fangs. "I claim the right of battle. It's a matter of honor."

Pepper's eyes fluttered open. She moaned and covered her wound with her slender fingers.

Garmood glared cold-eyed and lethal at Rafe. "Agreed. You've taken her blood and I'll punish you for it."

She struggled in Rafe's arms. "Put me down." He set her on her feet. She wobbled, but squared her slight shoulders. "Garmood, I accept."

"You can't." Rafe stepped between them. "I've bargained with Garmood and we've agreed. We'll fight."

"But you're hurt." Pepper latched onto his arm.

Garmood slid his wide mouth into a sly grin. "Kivronians ignore minor injuries. Last man alive takes Pepper as his mate, but I want something more." He lengthened his claws. "I keep Dante."

Rafe leveled his gaze on his red haired opponent. If Garmood won, he'd do what ever he wished. *I must subdue this monster.* "Dante isn't part of this. I want him released before we begin."

"You want." Garmood's yellow eyes turned hard as granite. "Really, Nucretah. The madness *has* tainted your mind. You have no say. What are you? Just a miserable warrior relegated to a puny planet to herd cattle. No one will miss you if I dispose of your worthless head. The President will commend me."

Rafe didn't engage the taunt. He'd listened to worse from the insanity in his head. Peace and clarity ruled his mind and strength flowed into his body, thanks to Pepper. Invulnerable power surged with each moment and every beat of his heart. Was it the return of what he'd lost to illness and would it prove enough to defeat Garmood?

CHAPTER FIFTEEN

Pepper watched, weak-kneed and shaking while the two warriors traded insults. As a reporter, she'd seen the Kivronian games from the cheap seats in the stadium, but she'd never witnessed at close range men intent on killing each other. And this time, her heart was invested. The contents of her stomach curdled. Her heart pounded. Loss of blood added light-headed fatigue.

Garmood appeared the obvious winner, superior height, breadth and weight, while Rafe owned determination, a rapidly healing body, and speed. David pitted against Goliath, but Rafe lacked a slingshot. It didn't bode well. The two vampires snarled like cats defending territory. Wicked claws glinted under fluorescent lights.

They rounded each other, a predatory dance to size up the opponent. Who would strike first? Garmood swiped at Rafe and missed his side by only inches. Rafe leapt back, slicing Garmood's jacket and baring the white-blue skin of his belly. They roared until the crates rattled and she thought her eardrums would burst. Pepper covered her ears with her hands, pinched her eyes shut, and sunk to the cold cement floor. How long would it go on?

A crash forced her eyes open. Her gaze fixed on arms and legs punching, kicking, taking turns shoving the other against the wall, and then the shelves. Boxes covered the floor. The combatants didn't seem to notice with their intent on destruction. They pulled away to square off again. Blood flowed from a gash on Garmood's jaw, another wound ripped the length of his arm. No telling what damage Rafe had sustained. Streaked with blood before the altercation, the fresh mingled with the old and colored him raw.

Another series of roars and they tangled on the ground, biting, gouging, grunting with each sharp twist of claws. They rolled and painted the concrete red. Pepper wanted to look away, but didn't dare. Any moment one man would rise victorious. It had to be Rafe.

They broke apart, panting, glaring, and alive. Intuition warned, screamed for her to act. Pepper, desperate to help Rafe, searched the enemy's sick mind for his next move. Too late. Garmood leaped on her, yanked her to her feet by her throat and shook her. She pulled at his fingers and gasped for air.

"Surrender or she dies." Garmood growled.

"Release her." Rafe stood, menacing and hard as steel. Her vision blurred.

Garmood laughed, extended one clawed finger and made a cut above her collarbone. Moisture trickled over her skin and onto her green dress. Her stomach knotted. Garmood flexed his fingers over her windpipe. "And why would I do that? I'm hungry."

Rafe launched himself in a blur of speed toward Garmood. Claws scraped her skin as the beast relinquished her neck and left her crumpled on the ground. Garmood toppled crates from the force of the blow, smashing them to the cement with explosive force. Debris and wood slats flew through the air like arrows. Pepper peeked around the safety of a metal shelf. Garmood gaped like a fish pinned to the wall, impaled by a shaft of wood, cut clean like an arrow to his broad chest.

"Look away, Pepper." Rafe voice was quiet, somber, and in control.

But she couldn't. Her curiosity insisted that she watch even knowing what he intended to do. A quick move, a violent slash and Rafe held Garmood's head in his hand by a hank of red hair.

# # #

Rafe stared at Garmood's remains, his huge body slumped on the wall, held up by the plank skewering him in place, and missing its identifying marker. The head dripped blood onto the cement and splashed onto Rafe's boots. *Another pair to be destroyed*. He wanted nothing more to remind him of his enemy. His scars were sufficient. "Pepper, I need a box."

She crawled out from behind the shelves, appearing fragile and shaken. Her auburn hair, a mass of curls gathering volume around her smudged face. Blood ruined her green dress. *My blood*. Pepper chewed at her lip like a frightened child and navigated with bare feet the minefield of debris, retrieved a cardboard container, and handed it to him. Staring at the ceiling while he worked to secure the prize, she rubbed her hands over her arms. "Can we leave?"

Rafe closed the lid over Garmood's severed head and tucked the box under his arm. Exhilaration, freedom, and strength coursed through his mind and body. The enemy had been dispatched and insanity exorcized, but total victory had been eluded. Pepper's shock had rocked him. He couldn't help what he'd done and it wasn't over. Dante must still be liberated. After he delivered the monster's head to the Council he could be either rewarded with promotion or exiled to one of the Kivronian outer moons. Pepper wouldn't enjoy that base existence. "This way."

They slipped through the door into the cool night, clear with a spray of stars to light their way. Rafe and Pepper stalked through the trees and met the ten-foot wall surrounding the fortress. He could vault over. "Pepper, climb on my back and hang on."

She wrapped her arms around his neck. "What are you doing?" Her voice quavered.

"Trust me."

She clutched him. He enjoyed the feel of her arms around his neck. With the box in tow, Rafe leapt, scaled the wall with Pepper's long legs dangling like a kite's tail in the wind. He looked around for a safe spot before hurtling down from the height and landing silently near scrub oak. Pepper pressed her body against his like a second skin. He peeled her off. Information was vital and there was no one else to ask. "I must find Dante. Did you read Garmood's thoughts?"

She hugged her arms around her middle. "He was supposed to be where I found you. I picked up bits, but there wasn't time to get much during the fight."

Discontent rumbled in Rafe's chest. "Anything."

"Dante's been moved."

"Is he alive?"

"He was."

The shrubs rustled. Rafe shoved Pepper behind him and bared his claws.

Bram stepped out of the woods. "You've looked better, brother. Where's Dante?"

Rafe relaxed his protective stance. "No idea."

Bram pulled his star dagger from his belt. "I'll just extract it from Garmood. Is he tied up nearby?"

"Dead," said Rafe, and opened the box of proof.

"Unlucky." Bram tightened his jaw and flexed his fingers. Rafe knew that look, irritation on a short fuse.

"Dante's not here." Pepper spoke up and latched on to Rafe. "I know he's in a dark place, maybe underground with a tall, blond man."

Bram narrowed his gaze to coals of smoldering rage. "Anthony?"

"Yes. That's the name." Pepper's fingers dug into Rafe's arm. "You know him?"

"Our *made* brother," said Rafe.

"Your brother? Then Dante's safe?"

"No, he's not," ground Bram.

CHAPTER SIXTEEN

The last two weeks flew by. They'd torn the fortress apart and searched Red Rock. With Bram's superior tracking skills and Pepper's intuition, they'd learned Dante had been spirited away to a dank prison in Rome. Anthony always preferred to bleed the family of resources from that location. Dr. Morgan had been ordered back to Kivron and Bram boarded the transporter to negotiate Dante's release.

Rafe shed his jacket and hung it on the hook near the front door. Bram had history with their *made* brother, and his form of negotiation would likely involve severing Anthony's appendages beginning with soft tissue. Anthony deserved whatever punishment Bram inflicted on him.

Enough of that *bogswipe*, Rafe had better things to occupy him. Pepper waited in her bedroom. The betrothal was over. Being pardoned for Garmood's execution, and his subsequent promotion to Lord of Earth's Security released some, but not all the tension he'd carried for weeks. Only one thing could cure his aching need and he meant to make the most of it.

Mounting the stairs two at a time, Rafe halted outside the

door. *Control yourself, man.* He'd gained her trust and now refused to ruin it with impetuous ardor. He couldn't throw her on the bed and take her like an animal. He felt like it, dreamed of having her rough, then gentle, and then all night long. He licked his lips, his body thrumming with desire. *Hold on. Patience.* He'd take his time—for her. "Darling." Rafe waited a moment and entered.

# # #

Pepper stood before the bed draped in a white robe, her hair, hanging damp and loose around her shoulders. She swallowed, certain that the warmth in her face had spread through her skin. His look of need made her pulse race, not with fear, but with anticipation. She loved him. Pepper loosened the front of her robe to welcome her husband.

"Come here," he said, his voice, a velvet seduction.

She stepped closer and Rafe slipped the terry cloth from her shoulders, letting it pool around her feet. His gaze traveled over her, eyes smoldering with appreciation. He cupped her face with his strong hands. "You're exquisite."

Pressing his mouth to hers, he teased with his tongue. *Not the demanding assault I expected.* His kiss shook her with tender emotion. Pepper opened to him and enjoyed the feel of his soft lips, firm on her mouth, his tongue stroking. She slid her arms around his neck and leaned into his warmth. How she wanted him. His kiss deepened. She accepted all he had, giving all she had in return.

"I want you more than I've wanted any woman," he whispered against her mouth. He brushed his lips over her ear and down the sensitive skin of her throat. She tingled.

His thoughts joined with hers as his touch sent flames over her skin and sank into her flesh.

With quick motion, he ripped the clothes from his body, sending his tantalizing, spicy scent into the air. She breathed him in. Her fingers clung to his back as he laid her on the bed and took her mouth with force, a command to yield. She surrendered. Wave after wave of bliss washed over and through her. Nothing had ever come close to the passion welling up inside, exploding through her heart, and searing her insides. Arms and legs, mouths and hands, frantic to touch and taste, all molding together in hunger and love. Fusing two into one body, one mind, one soul.

Hours later, he cradled her to him and pressed soft kisses over the top of her head. "You're mine, darling--forever."

Pepper nuzzled against his chest, finally safe and

contented. "That works both ways." Her walls weren't broken down. She'd removed them to accept the one man worthy of her trust and affection. She loved Rafe with fierce loyalty. She caught the smile that flitted over his lips, before she closed her eyes in sated exhaustion. "Forever."

# # #

Rafe watched her drift to sleep. This courageous girl had released him from torment, brought him peace and the future he longed for. And love. He'd never expected to adore her. Even if Dr. Morgan's experiments failed and they couldn't have children, he'd be happy holding her in his arms and sharing life with her. At some point, he'd transform his bride, and she'd join the ranks of *made* vampires, ensuring their eternity together. But when would remain her choice.

Rubbing one of her shiny curls between his fingers, he relished the feel and this season of calm. It wouldn't last. Revolution threatened. Lines were being drawn and sides taken between the battle for human freedom and Kivronian survival. The *made* vampires outnumbered the *born* and their allegiance would sway the fights outcome. But what side would they fall on? Rumors persisted that the *made* manipulated human rebels and might join with them. Pepper would sympathize with humanity. And soon, Rafe would have to make his own decision. He planted a kiss on her shoulder. She smiled in innocent bliss. He'd make his choice, but not tonight.

THE END

#

Thank you

for purchasing CONQUERED.

Watch for the second book in the Kivronian Vampire Series.

BETRAYED

Available in 2013

BETRAYED

Trust is required for betrayal to flourish.

Betrayal has made Bram a swaggering vampire with something to prove. Unfortunately, his opportunity for vindication arises when his brother is kidnapped by Bram's enemy and held in Rome's catacombs. If Bram fails to free him, his brother will suffer torture and die. Bram would never forgive himself. His only chance of success may be a human.

Beautiful Angela Russo, has polish, connections, and a grudge. The vampires have stripped her family of power and position, destroying their lives. Forgiveness isn't one of Angela's virtues. She is used to getting what she wants, and what Angela wants is revenge.

When Bram and Angela are forced into a reluctant alliance, the secrets they uncover shatter everything they have believed to be true.

Can they learn to forgive the past and work together before blood runs in the streets?

Enjoy the following excerpt

from the Greek Gods Series

APOLLO'S GIFT

~CHAPTER ONE~

Something drew Cassie Priam to Delphi. She'd always been enamored with Greece, read all the myths as a child, and had chosen Ancient Civilizations for her major in college. She trudged the trail, her hiking boots crunching with each step. The fragrance of cypress, wild flowers and sun-baked earth brought visions to her mind of another time. Ancient Greece, when seekers of knowledge had climbed Mount Parnassus to bring gifts to the oracle, and gain wisdom. Cassie often dreamed of the path she now trod, but those night visions centered in a time three thousand years ago when Apollo had ruled the spot.

The summer-blue sky welcomed her on this last visit to Apollo's temple. Tomorrow she'd fly home to Washington D.C.

and the task of getting her doctorate. Her dad didn't think much of digging in the dirt or poring over musty texts in Greek and Latin. He called it a youthful diversion. Time to grow up and enter the real world. What he meant was, his world. The violent political sphere where Washington politics and her dad's post as US Secretary of Defense made for tactical debates and power grabs, rather than the poetry of Homer or adventures of Greek gods.

Cassie stopped to adjust her wide-brimmed hat to protect her face from the Mediterranean sun. She preferred to go without the straw covering. Because she stubbornly refused to wear it, her olive skin had tanned to a deep bronze over the summer, and her mother would have plenty to say about the aging effects of her outdoor life. No point in arguing with her mother, Dr. Priam knew her stuff. Cassie would smile through her mother's helpful comments about her wild dark hair, and that no young women of twenty-five should continue in the style of her teens. But t-shirts, shorts, and no make-up suited Cassie. Why worry about style when you're out in the middle of nowhere with a bunch of dried-up archeologists, and a few students more interested in a two-thousand-year-old shard of pottery than in the latest fashion?

She opened her bottle of water and gulped. The cool liquid splashed over her lips, leaving drops, trickling down her neck and between her breasts. The temple wasn't much further. She'd come so often that she knew the path like her own features. Even in the dark, Cassie would be able to find the place where the oracle had long ago breathed in the toxic fumes that drugged her, induced an alternate reality and brought communion with the gods.

Odd, but she'd known the place before ever setting foot amid the columns, as if she belonged there. It had to be her studies, all the pictures of Delphi and the amphitheater above the temple stamped onto her mind. That's all it was, all it could be. While her friends spent their last day in Greece touring Athens, Cassie opted for Apollo's temple at Delphi. Not the grandest of ruins, destroyed and rebuilt over the ages, yet she couldn't escape the dreams that compelled her.

Turning off the Via Sacra path, she entered the temple site. Stone block walls lined the area, half tumbled and decayed. The foundation remained a footprint. When she closed her eyes she could imagine the grandeur of perfectly, chiseled pillars towering above her. And envision the carefully guarded crevice, the world's navel, where Apollo's Pythia had raved her prophecies.

Sun heated her khaki shorts, and lemon yellow t-shirt until sweat dampened them both, and also her energy. Cassie pulled off her hat, fanned herself with it, and moved into the protective shade of a secluded cypress tree. She sat on the ground amid the weeds and leaned back against a rock slab of decaying wall. Warmth leached from the stone into her bones. Staying up late packing and waking early to make her trek added to heat-induced drowsiness. Just a quick close of her eyes and she'd be ready to make her final observations.

# # #

Cassie squinted against harsh light. Shade replaced by scorching rays, she shielded her eyes from the glare with her hand and casted about for her hat. How long had she slept?

"Cassandra," said a male voice as smooth as silk.

She shifted her gaze in the direction of the voice and locked on to an incredibly handsome man standing beside a pillar. A mane of golden waves topped with a laurel wreath crowned his classic features, and accentuated eyes blue as the Mediterranean set against a golden tan. "I've been waiting for you."

Blinking, she focused on the exquisite masculine form. Not

a statue, but worthy of marble. "Um, you must have me mixed up with someone else." Some super model would garner his attention, but not her, definitely not her. She nabbed her hat off the ground and got to her feet.

He smiled, the kind that movie stars flashed and weakened more than a girl's knees. "There's no mistake. You're my Cassandra and I've brought you a gift."

He strode toward her, his muscles rippling with fluid movement. The man was beautiful, but apparently none too bright. "I'm not who you're looking for, and what's with the get-up?" She pointed to his toga. "Practicing for a Greek tragedy?"

He closed the distance between them. Even in the day's heat, she felt warmer with him near. His mouth tightened. "I wear the clothing of the gods."

Names from Greek mythology popped into her head. "You're too young for Zeus, and too blond for Hades." She crossed her arms over her chest. "Okay, so who are you?"

His gaze pierced through her like twin beams of cobalt light. "Apollo."

"Of course!" Cassie slapped the side of her leg. "I should have known."

"Yes, you should have. And now, you remember me?"

"Are you kidding? I've studied ancient Greek myths and found Apollo quite interesting. But why don't you drop this role-playing and tell me your real name?"

Fire flashed in his pale blue eyes. "Phoebus Apollo. Son of Zeus. God of light and prophecy, among other things."

"You're fantastic, so imperious and arrogant. Much better than the actor I saw in Athens."

"Actor?"

"Yes. He lacked your commanding presence."

"I *am* Apollo." The ground quaked, knocking her to the earth. "And you are Cassandra, my priestess, Pythia of Delphi and my consort."

The ground continued to shake. The man's body lifted up and hovered four feet above her, glowing like a lit candle. She cowered beneath his stern glare, awaiting the god's wrath.

Nothing happened.

Cassie glanced about, no thunderbolts streaked across the sky, and no fissure gaped to swallow her whole. A few termers put her off balance, but they weren't worthy of panic. *Get hold of yourself.* This had to be a dream. Any minute she'd wake. And since it was a dream, she might as well enjoy it. *Why not have a little fun?* "Great Apollo, what is your will?" She did her best to sound serious and bowed low.

He floated like a cloud, waved his hand, and the ground stopped shaking. "I've come to give you a gift."

"Beware of Greeks bearing gifts," she murmured. "Thank you for the offer, but I couldn't possibly accept."

"It is my will." Another tremor sent her to all fours, her knees striking rough stone.

"Fine." She shifted to her bottom and rubbed a red patch on her knee. "What is it?" *This better be a dream.*

He landed beside her, his white robes fluttering in the breeze. "The greatest of all gifts, prophecy."

She glared at the dream masquerading as Apollo. "Oh, no. That never turns out well."

"I admit, that in your previous incarnation things didn't go as I'd planned, but I've negotiated with Hades, and paid a high price so your soul could take form in this body. You're my Cassandra, Princess of Troy."

This dream was fast becoming a nightmare. "Are you kidding? That was a disaster. Apollo gave Cassandra the gift of prophecy and then cursed her so no one believed her warnings. I think I'll pass."

"No, faithless, mortal woman. The curse came by way of your lie. You promised me your virtue and then spurned me." His honeyed voice had taken on a definite edge.

"Hey, not me. Cassandra was murdered ages ago." *Wake up, Cassie. Wake up.*

"Hear me." He stroked her hair with the tips of his fingers. She wanted to move away, but couldn't, his soft seductive tone freezing her in place. "You have a chance to make amends and give what is rightfully mine. Honor your promise to me and all will be well."

"You mean, be your consort."

"You are still pure."

"Well, that's none of your business." Heat rushed into her face. She'd had a number of short-lived boyfriends. They had all disappeared before things progressed to sex, and being dumped without explanation had done a number on her self-esteem. Cassie had convinced herself those relationships weren't right. Someone special waited for her and she would recognize him instantly, until then, she focused on her education. She stood, brushed the dirt from her shorts, and glanced at him from the corner of her eye.

"I am a god and discern that you haven't known a man." A

satisfied smile spread across his full, perfect lips. "I am pleased."

"Right," she grumbled. Dream or nightmare, the man was exasperating.

"You doubt me."

This had gone on too long. "Enough all ready. You're part of a dream brought on by hot sun and a romantic location, nothing to take seriously."

At least six-foot-five, he towered over her like an ionic column. He moved closer, pressing her against a crubling, stone wall. Her heart thumped in response. *He's a dream, a deliciously tempting dream.*

He leaned in, his mouth a kiss away. "I'm real and eternally serious." His breath smelled of nectar.

She licked her suddenly dry lips. Maybe she was wrong and this wasn't a nightmare, but a really, really good dream.

"This is no dream." He brushed his lips over hers, soft, warm, and as addictive as the fabled ambrosia. She leaned in wanting more, but he denied her. "It's done."

"What's done?" she murmured.

"The gift is given."

"No. Wait."

"Once given, I can't take it back."

Panic tightened her chest. *It's a dream. Damn. It better be a dream.* But what if it weren't? "I won't use it. Prophecy or not, nothing can make me tell people."

That beautifully irritating smile spread over his mouth. "Ah, Cassandra, you haven't changed. The same argument you tried in your last incarnation. I've missed this."

"Ugh." She stomped her foot. "I refuse."

He tilted his golden head and studied her. "I think not. It's against your nature to leave thousands to die when you have the ability to warn them."

She squared her shoulders. "This is not the city of Troy and I'm not your dead princess. Even if this gift were real, which it's not, no one would listen to me. People don't believe in prophecy these days. They'll shoot me full of meds and lock me in a rubber room."

His eyes softened. "Millions will suffer if you don't try."

"Millions?" Definitely a nightmare.

# # #

Cassie opened her eyes and stretched. What an odd dream and the man was disturbingly familiar. It couldn't have lasted more than a few minutes. "Apollo, really," she muttered. It would figure that the guy she'd been waiting for was a figment of her imagination. Her gaze fell to her hat lying beside her, a wreath of laurel laid over the wide brim.

"Damn."

Available in the fall of 2012

ABOUT THE AUTHOR

Sandy L. Rowland is an award-winning author who lives in the shadow of the Wasatch Mountains, and the twisted forms of the red desert with her loving husband and family. She craves adventure. Whether spending time in a sweat lodge in Southern Utah, living in a teepee for a month in New Mexico, or visiting the streets of Rome, she believes life is to be experienced.

You can learn more about Sandy and her books at:

www.sandylrowland.weebly.com

www.ingramcontent.com/pod-product-compliance
Lightning Source LLC
Chambersburg PA
CBHW030035180626
46810CB00001B/379